Among
the Barons

Among the Barons

MARGARET PETERSON HADDIX

ALADDIN PAPERBACKS
NEW YORK LONDON TORONTO SYDNEY

First Aladdin Paperbacks edition September 2004

Text copyright © 2003 by Margaret Peterson Haddix

ALADDIN PAPERBACKS
An imprint of Simon & Schuster
Children's Publishing Division
1230 Avenue of the Americas
New York, NY 10020

Also available in a Simon & Schuster Books for Young Readers hardcover edition.
Designed by Greg Stadnyk
The text of this book was set in Elysium.

Printed in the United States of America
10 9 8 7 6 5 4 3 2 1

The Library of Congress has cataloged the hardcover edition as follows:
Haddix, Margaret Peterson.
Among the Barons / Margaret Peterson Haddix.
p. cm.
Sequel to: Among the betrayed.
Summary: In a future world of false identities, government lies, and death threats, Luke feels drawn to the younger brother of the boy whose name Luke has taken.
ISBN 0-689-83906-5 (hc.)
[1. Brothers—Fiction. 2. Science fiction.] I. Title.
PZ7.H11135 Am 2003
[Fic]—dc21
2002004534
ISBN 0-689-83910-3 (pbk.)

For my father

CHAPTER ONE

"**H**ey, L.! Mr. Hendricks wants to see you!"

Such a summons would have terrified Luke Garner only a few months earlier. When he'd first come to Hendricks School for Boys, the thought of having to talk to any grown-up, let alone the headmaster, would have turned him into a stammering, quaking fool desperately longing for a place to hide.

But that was back in April, and this was August. A lot had happened between April and August.

Now Luke just waved off the rising tide of "ooh's" from his friends in math class.

"What'd you do, L.? Have you been sneaking out to the woods again?" his friend John taunted him.

"Settle down, class," the teacher, Mr. Rees, said mildly. "You may be excused, Mr., uh, Mr. . . ."

Luke didn't wait for Mr. Rees to try to remember his name. Names were slippery things at Hendricks School anyway. Luke, like all his friends, was registered under a different name from what he had grown up with. So it was always hard to know what to call people.

Luke edged his way past his classmates' desks and slipped out the door. His friend Trey, who had delivered the message from Mr. Hendricks, was waiting for him.

"What's this about?" Luke asked as the two fell into step together, walking down the hall.

"I don't know. I just do what he tells me," Trey said with a dispirited shrug.

Sometimes Luke wanted to take Trey by the shoulders, shake him, and yell, "Think for yourself! Open your eyes! Live a little!" Twelve years of hiding in a tiny room had turned Trey into a human turtle, always ready to pull back into his shell at the slightest hint of danger.

But Mr. Hendricks had taken a liking to Trey and was working with him privately. That was why Trey was running errands for him today.

Trey looked furtively over at Luke. His dark hair hung down into his eyes. "Do you suppose it's—you know—time?"

Luke didn't have to ask what Trey meant. Sometimes it seemed like everyone at Hendricks School was just holding his breath, waiting. Waiting for a day when none of the boys would be illegal anymore, when they could all reclaim their rightful names, when they could go back to their rightful families without fear that the Population Police would catch them. But both Luke and

Trey knew that that day wouldn't come easily. And Luke, at least, had promised to do everything he could to bring it about.

His stomach churned. The fear he thought he'd outgrown reached him at last.

"Did he say . . . did Mr. Hendricks say . . . ," he stammered. What if Mr. Hendricks had a plan for Luke to help with? What if that plan required more courage than Luke had?

Trey went back to looking down at the polished tile floor.

"Mr. Hendricks didn't say anything except, 'Go get your buddy L. out of math class and tell him to come see me,'" Trey said.

"Oh," Luke said.

They reached the end of the hall, and Luke pushed open the heavy wood door to the outside. Trey winced, as he always did anytime he was exposed to sunshine, fresh air, or anything else outdoors. But Luke breathed in gratefully. Luke had spent his first twelve years on his family's farm; some of his fondest memories involved the feeling of warm dirt on his bare feet, sunshine on the back of his neck, a hoe in his hand—and his parents and brothers around him.

But it didn't do to think much about his parents and brothers anymore. When he'd accepted his fake identity, he'd had to leave them and the farm behind. And even when he'd been with them, he'd had to live like a shadow or a ghost, something no one else outside the family knew about.

Once when his middle brother, Mark, was in first grade, he'd accidentally slipped and mentioned Luke's name at school.

"I had to tell the teacher that Mark just had an imaginary friend named Luke," Luke's mother had told him. "But I worried about that for months afterward. I was so scared the teacher would report you, and the Population Police would come and take you away. I'm just glad that a lot of little kids do have imaginary friends."

She'd bitten her lip telling Luke that story. Luke could still see the strained expression on her face. She hadn't even told him about that episode until the day before he left the farm and his family for good. By then she'd meant the story as assurance, he knew—assurance that he was doing the right thing by leaving.

At the time, Luke hadn't known what to make of that story. It just added to the jumble of confused thoughts and fears in his head. But now—now that story made him angry. It wasn't fair that he'd had to be invisible. It wasn't fair that his brother couldn't talk about him. It wasn't fair that the Government had made him illegal simply because he was a third child and the Government thought families should have no more than two.

Luke stepped out into the sunshine feeling strangely happy to be so angry. It felt good to be so sure about what he thought, so totally convinced that he was right and the Government was wrong. And if Mr. Hendricks really did have a plan for Luke, it'd be good to hang on to this righteous anger.

The two boys climbed down an imposing number of marble steps. Luke noticed that Trey glanced back longingly at the school more than once. Not Luke. Hendricks had no windows—to accommodate the fears of kids like Trey—and Luke always felt slightly caged anytime he was inside.

They walked on down the lane to a house half hidden in bushes. Mr. Hendricks was waiting for them at the door.

"Come on in," he said heartily to Luke. "Trey, you can go on back to school and see about learning something for once." That was a joke—Trey had done nothing but read while he'd been in hiding, so he knew as much about some subjects as the teachers did.

Luke opened the door, and Mr. Hendricks rolled back in his wheelchair to give Luke room to pass. When he'd first met Mr. Hendricks, Luke had been awkward around him, particularly because of the wheelchair. But now Luke practically forgot that Mr. Hendricks's lower legs were missing. Going into the living room, Luke automatically stepped out of the way of Mr. Hendricks's wheels.

"The other boys will find this out soon enough," Mr. Hendricks said. "But I wanted to tell you first, to give you time to adjust."

"Adjust to what?" Luke asked, sitting down on a couch.

"Having your brother here at school with you."

"My brother?" Luke repeated. "You mean Matthew or Mark . . ." He tried to picture either of his rough, wild older brothers in their faded jeans and flannel shirts walking up the marble stairs at Hendricks. If he felt caged at the windowless school, his brothers would feel handcuffed, pinned down, thoroughly imprisoned. And how could Mother and Dad possibly afford to send them here? Why would they want to?

"No, *Lee*," Mr. Hendricks said, stressing the fake name that Luke had adopted when he'd come out of hiding. Luke knew that he should be grateful that the parents of a boy named Lee Grant had donated his name and identity after the real Lee died in a skiing accident. The Grants were Barons—really rich people—so Luke's new identity was an impressive one indeed. But Luke didn't like to be called Lee, didn't like even to be reminded that he was supposed to be somebody else.

Mr. Hendricks was peering straight at Luke, waiting for Luke to catch on.

"I said your brother," Mr. Hendricks repeated. "Smithfield William Grant. *You* call him Smits. And he's coming here tomorrow."

CHAPTER *TWO*

Mr. Hendricks handed Luke a picture, but Luke was too shocked to look at it yet.

"Lee's brother," he finally said quietly. "Lee's brother is coming to school here. Tomorrow."

"Yes, your brother," Mr. Hendricks repeated. "*You* are Lee."

"Aw, Mr. Hendricks," Luke protested. "It's just you and me. We don't have to pretend, do we? And the other kids—they *know* I'm not really Lee Grant. This Smits kid is going to know I'm not his brother. So we don't have to act like it, do we?"

Mr. Hendricks just looked at Luke. Luke couldn't stop the flow of questions. "Why's he coming here, anyway?"

"He misses his older brother," Mr. Hendricks said. "He misses you."

The "older" was a surprise. Luke felt even stranger now.

"Mr. Hendricks, I never even knew Lee had a brother. This kid couldn't miss me. He's never met me. What's really going on here?"

Mr. Hendricks seemed to sag a bit against the back of his chair.

"I'm only repeating what his parents told me over the phone this morning," he said.

"Well, of course," Luke said. "They know it's not safe to say anything real over the phone. They know the Population Police tap phone lines all the time. This is all some . . . some mix-up or something."

"Luke—Lee, I mean—I don't really know what's going on here. But I think it's best to proceed with caution. You do need to begin acting like Lee. You do need to pretend that you know Smits well, as a brother. For the sake of everyone involved."

Usually Luke had a lot of respect for Mr. Hendricks, but now he couldn't resist making a face.

"That's crazy," Luke said. "Why pretend when nobody's going to be fooled?"

"Nobody?" Mr. Hendricks countered. "Nobody? Don't be so sure. Actors can't always know who's in the audience."

Luke shook his head disdainfully.

"This is Hendricks School," he said. "This isn't Population Police headquarters. This isn't some Government convention. We're safe here. Everyone knows we're almost all third children with fake I.D.'s. Nobody's going to report us."

"Really," Mr. Hendricks said. "Is your memory that short? What about Jason?"

Jason had been a Population Police spy who'd infiltrated

the school. Just hearing his name could still send a shiver of fear through Luke's body, but he held it back, tried not to let Mr. Hendricks see.

"Jason's gone now," Luke said. He was proud of the way he kept his voice level and calm. "And you said yourself, you're screening new applicants better, you're not going to let that happen again. And we're all so . . . comfortable here now. We're talking to one another about being illegal, about having fake I.D.'s. We're all friends."

Mr. Hendricks rolled over to the window and stared out at a cascade of forsythia that hid his house from the lane.

"I worry that you've all become too comfortable. That we're not preparing you for . . ." He let his voice trail off. Then he looked back at Luke. "For reality. What if this Smits is another Jason?"

The question hung in the air. To escape Mr. Hendricks's gaze, Luke glanced down at the photo of Smits. He saw cold gray eyes, a patrician nose, light hair, a sneer. Smits Grant was probably only eleven or twelve years old, but he might as well have been a miniature adult. The look he had given the camera—and now seemed to be giving Luke— made Luke feel like a poor, dumb country kid again. Never mind that Luke himself was wearing leather shoes, tailored pants, and a fancy shirt and tie. He felt barefoot, snotty-nosed, and ignorant beyond words, compared with the photo of Smits.

"Can't you tell him not to come?" Luke asked Mr.

Hendricks. "Say he's not allowed at your school? If you're worried, I mean."

"He's Smithfield *Grant*," Mr. Hendricks said. "His father—your father—is one of the most powerful men in the country. I'd have a better chance of stopping the wind than stopping a Grant from doing what he wants."

"I'm a Grant, too," Luke said. He wasn't sure whether he was trying to make a joke or trying out the words, trying to make them sound true. His voice came out limp and uncertain, failing on all accounts.

But Mr. Hendricks nodded.

"Good," he said. "Remember that."

CHAPTER *THREE*

Luke sat at the top of the steps that led to Hendricks School. Smits Grant was due to arrive any minute, and Luke had already begun his charade.

My brother's on his way, Luke told himself. *I'm so excited, I couldn't wait inside. I couldn't stand it if I weren't the first one to see him.*

Nothing could have been further from the truth. Mr. Hendricks had all but threatened Luke with a firing squad just to get him outside. As far as Luke was concerned, he'd be happy if he *never* saw Smits.

Could that happen? What if Luke turned around now, hid inside, and somehow managed to stay out of Smits's way forever? They ought to have different classes. Luke could find out the other boy's schedule and make sure their paths never crossed. Luke had plenty of experience hiding.

Of course, to avoid Smits he'd also have to go without eating. All the boys always ate together, in the dining hall.

Luke just couldn't see Mr. Hendricks agreeing to let Luke eat somewhere else.

And he didn't want to. *His* friends would all be eating in the dining hall. What he really wanted was for Smits to be the one set apart, hidden. That is, if he had to be at Hendricks at all.

For perhaps the billionth time since he'd learned about Smits, Luke wondered, *Why in the world would he want to come here?*

Luke kept his eyes on the long, curving driveway. A dark car turned in at the Hendricks School gates, disappeared behind a clump of trees, reappeared, and sped on toward the school. Luke's stomach churned.

The car pulled up in front of the school. It seemed about as long as a tractor and a hay wagon combined. The windows—all ten of them—were tinted black, so Luke couldn't tell if there was a boy inside staring out just as intently as Luke was staring in.

Oh, no. What if Smits's parents had come, too?

Luke hadn't thought of that before. Now panic coursed through his veins. He couldn't meet all three Grants at once. He just couldn't.

The driver's door glided open—smoothly, like it was on oiled hinges. Luke held his breath, waiting to see who would appear. A polished boot stepped out, followed by a second one that seemed even shinier. Then a tall, aristocratic-looking man in a dark blue uniform and stiff cap stood up. The uniform had gold braid around the cuffs and collar, and at the rim of the cap. Luke could even have believed it was real gold, pure metal.

The man turned and practically marched, soldierlike, to the other side of the car. He opened a second door, held out his hand, and said, "Sir?"

So this wasn't Mr. Grant. This was a servant. A chauffeur.

Luke could see a very pale hand thrust out of the car and clasp the chauffeur's. Then a boy stepped out. Luke recognized him from the picture of Smits Grant.

Somehow Luke managed to make his feet maneuver down the stairs, toward the car. Mr. Hendricks had made it quite clear: Luke *had* to act eager to see Smits. He had to rush over to him right away. But Luke's mind was racing faster than his feet.

What am I supposed to do when I get there? Shake his hand? Or—oh, no. What if the Grants are the type of family who hug one another?

Luke stumbled at the bottom of the stairs but caught his balance again quickly. He didn't think the chauffeur or Smits even noticed. They weren't looking toward Luke. Luke planted his feet a mere yard from the younger boy, but he had to clear his throat before Smits turned his head toward Luke.

"Hi, uh, Brother," Luke said awkwardly.

He lifted his right arm tentatively, to shake hands if that's what Smits wanted to do. Or if Smits stepped close enough and reached out, Luke could probably force his arms to wrap around Smits in something like a hug. If he had to.

Smits didn't move.

His cold gray eyes looked straight at Luke—straight through him, it almost seemed. For a horrible second Luke was afraid that Smits was going to refuse to acknowledge him, maybe even yell out, "This boy's a fraud! He stole my real brother's name!" Then Smits's gaze flickered away, and he mumbled, "Hey, Lee."

Luke exhaled, only barely managing not to let out an audible sigh of relief.

Smits looked at the chauffeur.

"My luggage?" he asked.

"Of course, sir," the chauffeur said, and walked to the back of the car.

Luke let his half-extended right arm fall back to his side. It was clear that Smits didn't want Luke to touch him. While Smits was watching the chauffeur, Luke got the nerve to peer past him, into the car. If Mr. and Mrs. Grant were in there, he wanted to be prepared.

"They didn't come," Smits said.

Luke jumped. "Huh?"

"Mom and Dad," Smits said. "They had no interest in accompanying me here." He sounded so smug saying that, Luke wanted to punch him.

"Oh," Luke said. "Well, why would they?" He was

trying to sound casual, the way he would with his own brothers. His real brothers.

"Because of *me*," Smits said. "Because they might have wanted to say good-bye to *me*."

CHAPTER *FOUR*

By dinnertime the rumors were flying through the school. The new boy had brought four suitcases, his own computer, and a giant TV. The new boy had taken one look at the room he was supposed to share with five other boys, stalked down to the office, and demanded a room of his own. A big one even. The new boy had wandered into the dining hall, gotten one whiff of the evening meal, and instantly ordered that all *his* meals be privately catered, brought in from the city, an hour away.

Luke was willing to believe any of those rumors. But as far as he knew, he was the only boy in the school who had actually met Smits.

"What's he really like?" Trey asked as he poked his fork at the tasteless heap of boiled greens on his plate. "Is he truly awful?"

Luke chewed for a minute and swallowed, glad for once that the food was so stringy and tough. It gave him time to think. He shrugged, trying for nonchalance.

"Well, he's my brother," Luke said. "Aren't most brothers awful?"

Trey snorted. "Your brother—right. So why didn't *you* bring a computer and a TV? Why don't *you* have a private room? Why are you eating this slop when you could be having—I don't know—caviar? Foie gras?"

Luke didn't have the slightest idea what caviar or foie gras was, but he wasn't about to admit it. He could feel the whole tableful of boys watching him, waiting for his response. He shrugged again.

"Guess I'm just not as picky as he is," Luke said. "Guess I'm a nicer person."

Luke was relieved that the other boys had stopped staring at him. Instead, their gaze was trained just beyond him, right over his head.

"Lee," someone said.

Luke whirled around and saw what the others were looking at. It was Smits. Luke felt his face go red. How much had Smits heard?

"Aren't you going to introduce me?" Smits asked coldly. He slid into a seat beside Luke. The other boys scrambled to make room for him, as if the table actually belonged to Smits and they were just grateful that he wasn't ordering them away entirely.

"Um, sure," Luke said. "Everybody, this is my brother, Smits." He was proud of himself that he could get the words of that colossal lie out of his mouth so smoothly. "Uh, Smits, this is Trey and, um, Robert and Joel and John. . . ."

Smits nodded after each name and reached out his hand for each boy to shake. After some fumbling, Luke's friends managed to think to stick their hands out as well. Luke wasn't surprised by his friends' awkwardness, but he felt strangely ashamed. Why couldn't Trey have remembered to put down his fork before he reached out his hand? He'd splashed some of the slimy greens right onto Smits's shirt. And Smits only made it worse, pretending not to notice, just shaking hands right and left, smooth as a politician.

"Nice to meet you," Smits said again and again. "Nice to meet you."

Luke remembered what he'd thought when he'd first seen the picture of Smits—that Smits looked like a miniature grown-up. He acted like one, too. Or like a little robot, programmed to say what some stiff, formal grown-up would want a kid to say. Luke had half a mind to yell at him, "Oh, knock it off. Tell us all the truth. Why are you here?"

But of course he didn't.

"So," Smits said when the introductions were finally over. "Is this a decent place? Lee here hasn't told me a whole lot. Doesn't write home as much as Mom wants him to." He gave Luke a playful punch on the arm and sort of winked at the rest of the boys. "I must say, I've found the staff quite accommodating."

Luke figured Trey was the only one at the table who knew what "accommodating" meant. That had to be the reason Trey actually opened his mouth.

"So they did let you have a private room," Trey said. "And get the food you want."

Smits looked down at the other boys' meals.

"Sure," he said. "Nobody could possibly be expected to eat *that*."

Luke saw Joel and John silently put their forks down.

"It's not so bad," Luke said. "You should give it a try before you make up your mind."

Smits laughed.

"No, thanks," he said. "Mom always did say you had an undiscriminating palate. Dad used to joke, 'Lee'll eat anything that doesn't eat him first.' *I'm* not like that."

"Nothing but the best for Smits, right?" Luke said quietly.

Smits clapped him on the back.

"You remembered!" he said. He shoved away from the table. "Well, I'll be off now. Just wanted to meet Lee's friends. See you all later."

And, in total defiance of school rules, he strolled out of the dining hall.

Nobody stopped him. Luke and his friends stared off after him for a full minute.

"What was that all about?" Trey said finally.

"I haven't the slightest clue," Luke said.

CHAPTER *FIVE*

They had games after dinner.

This was something that Luke was very proud of. It had been his idea to ask Mr. Hendricks for a time to run and play. Most of his friends, in hiding, had been in small spaces. They'd been trained from birth to be quiet and still, to whisper, not yell, to tiptoe, not run. Their lives had depended on it. Luke didn't know how many shadow children had ever been discovered because of a poorly timed squeal of joy or a scamper across a creaky floor. He didn't want to know. But his friends were so good at not moving, at not talking, that they sometimes seemed hidden even now.

"They need a chance to be kids," Luke had argued with Mr. Hendricks back at the beginning of the summer. "They need a time to run as fast as they can, to scream at the top of their lungs, to . . ." Luke hadn't been able to finish his sentence. He'd been overcome with the memory of all the games he'd played with his brothers—his real brothers.

Football, baseball, kickball, spud. Dodgeball, volleyball, kick the can, tag . . .

"All right," Mr. Hendricks had said. "You're in charge."

At first Luke's idea had seemed like a disaster. Boys who had sat still all their lives had no idea how to run. They cowered at the sight of a ball rolling toward them, collapsed in fear to see a football spiraling their way. But Luke had been patient, throwing the balls so slowly they barely seemed to move, applauding anyone who managed even to walk fast. And now, after three months, Trey had a pretty good pitching arm on him, and John was a master at dodgeball, and there was a little kid in the eight-year-old class who could run so fast, he could even beat some of the teachers who occasionally stayed for races.

Luke thought he had every right to be proud. They still mostly played in the dining hall, with all the tables and chairs cleared away, because the idea of going outside was too much for most of the boys. But Luke had hopes. By next summer, he thought, they'd all be outdoors climbing trees, maybe even making up games of their own.

That was what Luke dreamed of, when he wasn't dreaming of the Population Law being changed.

But tonight, as he began folding up chairs and tables after dinner, Ms. Hawkins, the school secretary, stopped him.

"No games for you tonight, young man," she said.

Luke gaped at her. Ms. Hawkins never stayed around school until dinnertime, let alone afterward. She was a shadowy figure herself—Luke couldn't remember her saying two words to him even once since the first day he'd arrived at school.

Ms. Hawkins went on talking, as if she was used to boys not answering. She probably was.

"You're to meet your brother in the front hallway instead," she said. When Luke didn't move, she snapped, "Now! Get on with you!"

Luke handed her the chair he was holding. She managed to grasp it but looked puzzled, as if she could no longer understand what it was just because it was folded up.

Except for Mr. Hendricks, all the staff at the school were a little strange. If Luke hadn't known better, he would have wondered if they'd all spent their childhood in hiding as well. But the Population Law had been in effect for only fourteen years; Luke was among the oldest kids to come out of hiding. Mr. Hendricks had just hired odd people on purpose.

"If Ms. Hawkins ever tried to turn any of you in," he'd told Luke once, "who would believe her?"

That was true of the teachers, too, and the school nurse. It was even true of the school janitor. Luke understood Mr. Hendricks's reasoning, but sometimes he longed to be around normal adults. He wasn't sure now what to believe of Ms. Hawkins's instructions. What if she was just confused? Shouldn't Smits be here playing games with the other boys, instead of pulling Luke away, too?

"Didn't you hear me?" Ms. Hawkins said threateningly.

"Um, sure," Luke said. "I mean, yes, ma'am."

He turned and walked toward the door.

"Trey, can you organize the games tonight?" he called to his friend on his way out.

"Wha—how do I do that?" Trey asked. He sounded as panicked as if Luke had asked him to attack Population Police headquarters.

"Get John to help. And Joel," Luke said.

Joel and John glanced up from the table they were folding. They looked every bit as stricken as Trey.

Luke had no confidence that they'd manage without him. But he pushed his way out the door anyhow.

The hall outside the dining room was quiet and dimly lit. Luke rushed past dark classrooms and offices. He'd just tell Smits to get lost—that's what he'd do. Smits had no right to order him around.

But when Luke got to the front hallway—an echoey place with ancient-looking portraits on the walls—his resolve vanished. Smits was standing there alone. He had his back to Luke, and for the first time Luke realized what a small boy Smits really was. From behind he looked like the kind of kid you'd pick last for a baseball team.

Then Smits turned around.

"Hey, bro," he said heartily. "I thought you might give me a tour of the school grounds. Let me see what this place is really like."

"Okay," Luke said hesitantly.

Smits was already pushing open the front door, as if he, not Luke, were the one who knew Hendricks School. They walked down the stairs in silence, then Smits turned around and regarded the building with narrowed eyes.

"Why aren't there any windows?" he asked.

Luke wondered how much Smits had been told about Hendricks, about third children, about the needs of kids coming out of hiding. Surely Smits knew the truth. Surely he didn't need to ask a question like that.

Luke opted for the safest answer possible anyhow.

"Some of the kids here have agoraphobia. Do you know what that is? It means they're afraid of wide-open spaces. Not having windows is part of the way Mr. Hendricks is trying to cure them," he said. "He thinks that if they can't see the outdoors, they'll start longing for it."

"But that's pretty much torture for the rest of us, isn't it?" Smits countered. "It's like cruel and unusual punishment. And it's a fire hazard." He shook his head, flipping hair out of his eyes. "I'm going to have a window installed in my room. Maybe in every room I'd ever be in. It wouldn't do to have the heir to the Grant fortune killed in a fire or something."

Luke noticed he said "heir," not "one of the heirs." Was that a clue? Was that why Smits had come—to warn Luke away from the family money? Was this Luke's cue to say, "Hey, I don't want a dime of your fortune. I don't want anything from your family. Just an identity. Just the right to exist"?

Luke didn't say anything. It was true, he didn't care about the Grants' money. But he couldn't bring himself to speak sincerely to this strange, overconfident kid. It was easier to keep pretending the lie between them was reality.

They started strolling down the driveway. In different company this would have been a pleasant walk. Crickets sang in the bushes; the sunset glowed on the horizon. But Luke was too tense to enjoy any of it.

"That's the headmaster's house over there," he said, pointing. He was just talking to break the silence. "It's where Mr. Hendricks lives. You won't see him around the school much. He kind of lets it run on its own."

"I've already talked to him four times today," Smits said.

"Oh," Luke said. A few months ago he wouldn't have had the nerve to say anything else. But now he ventured, "What about?"

"Important matters," Smits said. They walked on. Luke could tell Smits wasn't really paying attention to anything around them. Not the weeping willows draping gently toward the driveway, not the sound of the brook gurgling just beyond the school grounds.

"I already saw all this, driving in," Smits said impatiently. "Isn't there anything else?"

"There's the back of the school," Luke said. "That's where we have our garden. And the woods——"

"Show me," Smits said.

They turned around. Luke struggled to hide his reluctance. If he was proud of the school's nightly games, he was even prouder of the school garden. Under his direction the Hendricks students had planted it, weeded it, and coaxed it into its full glory all summer long. Luke could just imagine

Smits barely glancing at it, then sniffing disdainfully, "So?"

And the woods—the woods were a special place, too. Back in the spring, when Luke had first arrived at Hendricks, he'd found refuge in the woods. He'd made his first attempt at a garden in a clearing there. He'd dared to stand up to the impostor Jason there. He'd met girls from the neighboring Harlow School for Girls there—including his friend Nina, who, he was sure, would also someday help in ending the Population Law.

Luke knew he could never explain all of that to Smits. Smits had no right to hear any of it. He probably wouldn't even care. So the woods, to Smits, would just look like a scraggly collection of scrub brush and untended trees.

Silently seething, Luke led Smits off the driveway and along an overgrown path winding down toward the woods. Darkness was falling now. Maybe Smits would be satisfied if they just rushed by the woods and the garden, and Luke wouldn't have to listen to any of Smits's comments.

At the edge of the woods Luke turned around. "Here. This is it. The woods. Now you've seen it."

Smits didn't answer, just ducked under a low branch. He reached out and touched a tree trunk hesitantly, as if he were afraid it would bite.

"Do you come here a lot?" Smits asked.

"I used to," Luke said brusquely.

"I don't know anything about nature," Smits admitted. "Sometimes I wonder . . ."

"What?" Luke asked.

Smits shook his head, as if unwilling or unable to say more. His fingers traced a pattern on the bark. He looked back toward Luke. In the twilight his face seemed paler than ever.

"Can you help me?" he whispered. "Can you be Lee?"

CHAPTER SIX

Luke stared at the younger boy.

"I—I don't know," he admitted. It was probably the first honest thing he'd said to Smits. "I can try."

Smits dropped his gaze.

"There's something wrong with the way he died," he whispered. Luke had to lean in close to hear.

"He was skiing, wasn't he?" Luke asked. Luke had only the faintest idea of what skiing was. "Did he run into a tree or something?"

Smits shook his head impatiently.

"You don't understand," he said. "He—" Smits broke off, his gaze suddenly riveted on something far beyond Luke. Then he snapped his attention down to the ground and raised his voice. "Ugh! Why did you bring me here! Now my shoes are all muddy!"

Baffled, Luke glanced over his shoulder. A burly man Luke had never seen before was running down the hill toward them.

"I see you, Smithfield," the man yelled. "Your game is up."

The man came closer. It was like seeing a tree run, or a mountain—the man was that imposing. Luke could only watch in awe. The man had muscles bulging from his arms and legs. His neck looked thicker than Luke's midsection. He had his fists clenched, as if he was ready to fight. Luke felt instant pity for any opponent this man might face.

"Hello, Oscar," Smits said, his voice as casual as it had been back in the dining room, greeting all of Luke's friends. He suddenly seemed like the little robot again.

"It is not funny, what you did," the man—Oscar—raged. "I have fully informed your parents. They are not amused, either."

Smits shrugged.

"Having a bodyguard is very tiresome, you know," Smits said.

For a minute Luke was afraid that Oscar was going to slug Smits. The huge man stepped closer, but he did nothing more threatening than narrowing his eyes.

"It is necessary," Oscar huffed. "It is not safe for you to go anywhere without protection. Especially"—he gazed distastefully around him, taking in the scrubby trees, the tall, untrimmed grass at the edge of the woods—"especially someplace unsecured like this."

"Well," Smits said. "Here's Lee. Why aren't you protecting Lee, too?"

Oscar's gaze flickered toward Luke, then back to Smits. His glare intensified.

"Your parents hired me solely to protect you," Oscar said. "I do my job with honor and dignity and pride." He spoke so pompously, Luke almost expected Oscar to snap into a military salute.

Smits was rolling his eyes.

"So you say. 'Honor and dignity and pride,'" he repeated, making a total mockery of the words. "You must have had a hard time explaining why you woke up hours late this morning, locked in your closet, when I had already left."

"I blame you!" Oscar exploded. "Your parents blame you! I told them the whole story. You drugged me and dragged me into that closet."

Luke decided he'd totally underestimated Smits if Smits had managed to drag Oscar so much as an inch. Smits would not be the last kid picked for a baseball team. He'd be the kid who could trample every other player, even without teammates.

"Me?" Smits said innocently. "I'm just a little kid. Where would I get anything to drug you with? How could I drag you anywhere?"

"You had help." Oscar growled. "The chauffeur—"

"Hey"—Smits shrugged again—"it's your word against his. And mine."

"But your parents believe me," Oscar retorted. He grabbed Smits's arm and jerked him practically off his feet.

"Come along. Let's get you somewhere safe."

"Fine," Smits said. "You can wipe the mud off my shoes when we get back to my room."

Oscar grunted.

Luke followed the other two up the hill. He kept a few paces behind. Smits seemed to have forgotten about him; Oscar had barely noticed him in the first place. Smits was now keeping up a running banter, making fun of Oscar for being muscle-bound and stupid and easily tricked.

What kind of a game was Smits playing? And—was it really a game?

Luke remembered the urgency in the other boy's voice. "Can you help me? Can you be Lee?" And, "There's something wrong with the way he died." What had Smits meant?

Luke thought he'd been escaping danger when he took Lee Grant's identity. Why did he suddenly feel like he'd only traded one peril for another?

CHAPTER SEVEN

It turned out that Smits did have classes with Luke—every single one of them.

"See, this is what happens when the big brother goofs off, runs away from school, and gets left behind a grade," Smits said, slipping into a desk beside Luke the next morning. "He gets stuck with his younger brother every minute of the day."

Luke could feel all his friends watching them. Smits beamed happily back at everyone.

"*I'm* the smart one in the family, in case you couldn't tell," Smits said.

Luke glowered. "Knock it off," he muttered under his breath.

"Someone's listening," Smits hissed back.

Luke half turned. At the back of the classsroom, barely two feet away, a hulking presence towered over all the boys still scurrying into the room.

Oscar.

MARGARET PETERSON HADDIX

Luke wasn't the only one staring. The huge man was enough of a sight to attract attention just by himself. But he stood out even more today because of what he held in his massive fists: a sledgehammer.

"Hey, everyone. Meet my bodyguard," Smits said.

"Is he always, um"—Trey gulped—"*armed* like that?"

"You mean the hammer?" Smits asked. He made a mocking face. "That's my parents' idea of a compromise. He'll be carrying that around until Mr. Hendricks installs a few windows." Smits looked around at blank expressions. "Didn't any of you ever think about what would happen if there was a fire here? How trapped you'd all be? You won't have to worry now. Hey, *your* parents should be chipping in on Oscar's wages, too. He'd be saving you guys, too, knocking down walls."

Smits pretended to swing an imaginary hammer himself.

From the front of the room Mr. Dirk, the teacher, said mildly, "Boys, we've always had plans in place for emergency evacuation procedures."

Everyone turned to stare in amazement at Mr. Dirk. Luke wondered if any of his friends had ever thought to worry about a fire before. The danger outside the walls of Hendricks School had always seemed so great, he was sure no one had ever feared being trapped inside. He felt like standing up and asking everyone, "Does it make you feel any better to have more to be scared of?"

Instead, he slid lower in his seat and kept quiet as Mr.

Dirk started lecturing about ancient history.

The rest of the day went about the same way. Smits made a spectacle of himself, Luke's classmates gaped at Oscar, and Luke could only slump lower and lower in his chair in each successive class. Meals should have been a relief, because Smits didn't show up for them. At least, not physically. But everyone in the dining hall seemed to be talking about him.

"What do you suppose *he's* eating right now?" Joel asked at dinner as thin gruel dribbled from his spoon.

"Roasted wild duck—illegally, I might add—garlic potatoes, French-cut green beans, and chocolate mousse," Trey said gloomily. "He told me."

"Maybe he was lying," Luke said.

"No," Trey said. "I believe him."

Luke did, too—about that. But he wasn't going to admit it.

"Hey, how much do you think his bodyguard has to eat to keep all those muscles?" John asked. "Did you see him? I couldn't do a bit of homework at study hour. All I could think about was what would happen if he swung that hammer at me. He was standing right behind me, you know."

"You never do any homework at study hour anyhow," Luke said. But nobody seemed to hear him.

By bedtime Luke just wanted the day to be over. But he'd barely fallen asleep before he woke to someone shaking him. It was a thick hand with muscular fingers. He'd never known before that people could have highly developed muscles in their fingers.

"Your brother needs you," a deep voice whispered. "Come on."

It was Oscar. Luke stifled a yelp of terror.

"Don't wake your roommates," Oscar warned.

Luke wondered if any of them were awake already but pretending to sleep. Seven other boys slept in his room. How many had their eyelids open, just a crack, just enough to watch Luke leave? If Oscar was luring Luke away to hurt him—to kill him, even—how many boys would be able to tell Mr. Hendricks, "Oscar came into our room at midnight to get Luke. It's Oscar's fault. Oscar's dangerous"?

Luke told himself Oscar had no reason to want to hurt Luke, let alone kill him. Luke had no reason to fear Oscar.

But he did anyway.

CHAPTER *EIGHT*

Luke forced himself to slide out of bed. Oscar kept a warning hand on Luke's shoulder, and it was all Luke could do not to grab Trey, who slept in the bunk bed above Luke, or Joel, who slept in the bed across from him, and beg, "Come with me! Protect me!" Luke suddenly felt like he needed a bodyguard, too.

But Luke kept silent, as if what mattered most was denying his own fear. Oscar propelled him out the door, into the hallway, and up a set of back stairs. Luke couldn't help remembering another time he'd been out of his room at night, and terrified. Then, he'd been desperate to thwart the plot of Jason, the Population Police spy who'd pretended to be another third child with a fake I.D. Now—did Oscar have a plot? Did Smits?

Luke reminded himself that, back then, he hadn't known if he could trust anybody at Hendricks. Now he could trust his friends, if he had to. He could trust Mr. Hendricks. He could run to any of the adults in the school, and even if they were strange, they would do their best to help him.

At the top of the stairs Oscar turned Luke toward a carved wooden door. Before Oscar even opened the door, Luke could hear someone crying behind it. As the door gave way Smits sat up in bed and stared resentfully at Luke.

"I miss . . ." he began. Whatever else he intended to say was lost in a wail of sorrow.

"Home," Oscar finished for him. "He's homesick. Acting like a stupid little kid."

Oscar sank into a chair at the end of the bed. He pushed Luke toward Smits. Smits's wail turned into keening. As Luke eased down onto the bed beside Smits he suddenly understood what Smits had intended to say. *Lee.* Smits missed Lee, the real Lee, the real older brother he must have looked up to and admired. And loved. For the first time Luke felt sorry for the younger boy. He couldn't imagine what it would be like to know that one of his real brothers, Matthew or Mark, was dead. It was bad enough that Luke would probably never see either of them again, but at least he could still think of them back home, playing pranks and baling hay, making fun of each other. Missing Luke. He could imagine their lives going on, even without him.

But Smits—Smits had nothing left of his brother. He was gone.

And Luke had taken his name.

Luke glanced fearfully back at Oscar. How could anyone hear Smits sobbing and think he was merely a foolish, homesick kid? Luke knew what grief was like. He could hear all the pain in Smits's wordless wails: *My brother is dead. I loved him and now he's gone, and I hurt more than I thought it was possible to hurt. . . .* What if Oscar suddenly understood, too?

Smits's grief was dangerous. Smits's grief could kill Luke.

Luke reached out and awkwardly patted Smits's shoulder.

"There, there," he said. His voice sounded wooden even to his own ears. "You're okay."

Smits stiffened. He looked at Luke in bewilderment, as if he'd never seen him before.

"Are you really homesick?" Luke asked. "Or did you just have a bad dream?"

Behind them Oscar turned on the overhead light. The harsh glare hurt Luke's eyes. Smits blinked rapidly.

"I guess I just had a bad dream," he said. "I—I dreamed you died."

"Well, I should hope you were crying, then," Luke said, trying to make his words sound like a joke between brothers, not a warning between strangers. "Go back to acting," Luke wanted to tell Smits. "Don't let Oscar know the truth. Don't you know what's at risk here?" But he wasn't sure that Smits did know. He wasn't sure that Smits cared.

Smits sniffed.

"Can I tell you the dream?" he asked.

Luke stole another quick glance at Oscar, who was now practically reclining in his chair, his eyes half closed. His very posture seemed to say, "Hey, I'm just supposed to guard the kid's body. Bad dreams aren't my problem."

"Sure," Luke said. "Tell me your dream."

"Y-you were skiing," Smits said. He stopped and gulped. He wouldn't look at Luke. He kept his head down, his eyes trained on his blanket. "You were skiing and you were in danger. You knew you were in danger—"

"What, were you skiing behind me?" Luke asked. "Was I scared you'd fall on me?" He was determined to keep this light, to keep Smits from descending back into that mad grief.

Smits flashed Luke a look of sheer fury. And Luke understood. Smits wasn't describing a dream. He was describing what had really happened to Lee. He thought Luke needed to know, and this was the only way Smits could tell him.

"I wasn't there," Smits said quietly. Luke wanted to protest, to say Smits was giving away too much now. But dreams sometimes had that kind of logic, that the dreamer could know things that happened far away.

"Did L—I mean, did I know what the danger was?" Luke asked.

Smits tilted his head thoughtfully.

"I don't know," he said. "Probably. You were carrying something. You weren't just skiing for fun. You were trying to get somewhere, to deliver something. And then a soldier shot you."

"A soldier?" Luke asked. He was used to fearing the Population Police. He'd never thought about soldiers hurting ordinary people.

Of course, the real Lee Grant had never been an ordinary person. He'd been the son of one of the richest men in the country.

"Why would a soldier want to shoot me?" Luke asked.

"I don't know," Smits said. He was crying again, but quietly. "He wanted to stop you from going wherever you were going. From delivering whatever you were delivering."

"And you don't know what that was? Or where I was going?"

Silently Smits shook his head.

Behind them Oscar suddenly released a giant snore. Luke jumped. Oscar's snores subsided into gentler rumblings. Smits giggled.

"Guess we don't have to worry about—," Luke started to say.

But Smits stopped giggling and clapped his hand over Luke's mouth. Then he leaned over and whispered in Luke's ear, "He might be faking. He's not as stupid as you'd think. He's always watching. . . ."

Smits backed away from Luke. The two boys stared at each other, trying to fit back into the roles they'd been playing.

"So that's all there was to your dream?" Luke said.

Smits nodded.

"So, see, it was just a nightmare. It wasn't real. I'm right here. Nothing happened to me. No soldier shot me. I wouldn't be skiing anyhow, this time of year."

With every word Luke spoke, he could see more tears welling up in Smits's eyes. Because, Luke knew, it was no comfort to Smits to have Luke there. It wasn't reassuring to know that Luke was alive. The real Lee was still dead.

"Here," Luke said roughly, patting Smits's pillow. "Just go back to sleep. You'll feel better in the morning."

Smits obediently slid down lower in the bed. But he didn't close his eyes.

"What's your favorite memory from when we were little kids?" Smits asked.

Luke hesitated. Then he said, honestly, "Having Mother tuck me into bed at night." He knew the real Lee had probably called his mother Mom, not Mother. But that didn't matter. This was one time when telling the truth wouldn't hurt.

Smits smiled drowsily. "Know what I remember? I remember when we got that big red wagon, and our nanny would pull us around in it, both of us together. Hour after hour. And then we got a little older, and you'd pull me in the wagon alone. Around and around the playroom. And I'd scream, 'Again! Again!' But I never pulled you. I should have pulled you, at least once . . ."

"You weren't big enough, stupid," Luke said. Smits

wasn't his real brother; Luke had never even seen that red wagon Smits was talking about. But Luke still had chills listening to him. "Tell you what. Next time we're anywhere near a wagon, you're welcome to pull me in it."

"It wouldn't be the same," Smits murmured. "It wouldn't be the same."

CHAPTER NINE

Mr. Talbot showed up the next day.

Mr. Talbot was the person who had helped Luke get his fake I.D. in the first place. Back when Luke was still in hiding, the Government had forced Luke's family to sell the woods behind their farm to build fancy houses for rich people. When the houses were finished, Mr. Talbot and his family had moved into the one closest to Luke's. Having other people so close by had terrified Luke's family; they were afraid that someone would discover Luke's existence. But instead Luke had discovered another third child in hiding: Mr. Talbot's daughter, Jen.

For several wonderful months Luke had secretly sneaked back and forth between his house and the Talbots'. Jen became his friend, and through an Internet chat room she introduced him to other third children in hiding. She also shared her dream with him, of a day when all third children could be free.

And then Jen was killed during a rally seeking that freedom.

Mr. Talbot had rescued Luke, given him Lee Grant's identity, and brought him to Hendricks School. Luke had seen him only twice since then—both times when there was danger.

And now he was back again. Just seeing him made Luke worry.

But the way Mr. Talbot acted, Luke could have believed that Mr. Talbot didn't have a care in the world. He breezed into Luke's science class and boomed out, "I'm sorry to interrupt—so sorry. I certainly believe that science is important, of course. But would anyone in here want to skip class to have lunch with me?"

In another classroom, at another school, Luke could imagine such an invitation causing kids to wave their arms in the air, screaming out, "Ooh! Ooh! I will! Pick me!"

But in Luke's class the boys froze. They stared warily at Mr. Talbot. Luke noticed that Smits was the only one who didn't look terrified. He narrowed his eyes and tilted his head thoughtfully. But even he didn't answer Mr. Talbot's question.

Mr. Talbot laughed heartily.

"Don't all jump at once," he joked. He turned to the teacher and said, "I see you have them all so entranced with science that they don't want to leave. I compliment you on the brilliance of your teaching."

The teacher, Mr. Nimms, looked every bit as frightened as his students.

"Well, I'm taking up too much of your time," Mr. Talbot said. "Mr. Hendricks really only has room for two boys at his table, and I promised the Grants I'd check up on their sons while I was here. Come on, Lee. Come on, Smits. Let's go have some gourmet food."

Luke heard somebody mumble resentfully, "Smits has that every day." Luke had to hide a grin as he, Smits, and Oscar stood up to leave.

"Oh, wait a minute," Mr. Talbot said. "You don't need to come." He was speaking to Oscar. "Mr. Hendricks has an excellent security system in his house, I assure you. Both of the Grant boys will be safe with me. You can take an hour off. I'm sure you'd be happy to have a break."

"My orders are to go wherever the boy goes," Oscar growled. "Always."

Luke had seen Mr. Talbot outsmart Population Police officers—not just once, but twice. He was sure Mr. Talbot would manage to twist Oscar's words around, twist his plans around, so that Oscar suddenly found himself agreeing, "Oh yes, yes, right. I will stay here. You go with the boys. I trust you."

But Mr. Talbot only shrugged.

"Your loss," he said. "I'll be sure to let your employers know how dedicated you are."

Luke was acutely aware of the presence of Oscar and Smits behind him as he walked beside Mr. Talbot out of the classroom, down the hall, then out the door toward Mr. Hendricks's house. Without them he could have been asking Mr. Talbot question after question: *Do you know why Smits is here? What are the Grants thinking? Is Smits dangerous? Can I trust him? And how did the real Lee die?* Mr. Talbot always had all the answers.

But today Mr. Talbot didn't seem to care about the questions in Luke's mind. He turned around and began talking to Smits.

"Have you adjusted to your new school yet?" Mr. Talbot asked. "Are you letting your parents know that everything's okay?"

"Why would they care?" Smits asked.

"Well, you are their son," Mr. Talbot said, still jovial.

"They liked Lee better," Smits said.

Oh, no. Had he really said "liked"—past tense? Luke's heart pounded as he panicked over what Oscar might have heard. He glanced over his shoulder. Oscar was trudging silently beside Smits, giving no sign that he'd heard anything at all.

"Oh, surely not," Mr. Talbot said quickly. "Surely they *love* you equally." Luke was grateful for the emphasis Mr. Talbot put on the present tense. "It must just seem like they prefer Lee right now, because Lee has done such a great job of turning his life around since he came to Hendricks. No more skipped classes, no more flunked courses—he's really applying himself. As I'm sure you'll apply yourself here, too."

"Whatever," Smits said.

They arrived at Mr. Hendricks's house, and Mr. Hendricks let them in.

"We're having a fine vegetable pot pie," Mr. Hendricks said. "With some of the peas and carrots and beans grown right here at the school, thanks to Lee."

Luke hoped that Smits heard the pride in Mr. Hendricks's voice, that Smits knew what Lee had accomplished. But Smits seemed to be off in his own little sullen world.

With Oscar standing guard behind them, they sat down at the dining-room table. At first there was a flurry of passing plates and dishing out servings. Then an uncomfortable silence fell over the table. Everybody seemed to be waiting for somebody else to speak. Finally Smits put down his fork.

"If you're here as my parents' messenger," Smits said, staring right at Mr. Talbot, "you can tell them they can't make me do anything."

"Ah," Mr. Talbot said. "And should I glare at them, just so, when I tell them that? I think the glare is an important part of the message, don't you?"

Smits glowered down at his plate and didn't reply.

"They're your parents," Mr. Hendricks said gently. "They care about you."

"They don't," Smits muttered.

"You know, I was once a boy like you," Mr. Hendricks said. "Selfish, only concerned with my own desires—"

"Selfish?" Smits exploded. "Selfish? Is it selfish to want to—" He broke off suddenly, looking from Oscar to Luke. Then he shoved his chair back from the table and turned and ran out of the room. Oscar was after him in a flash. Seconds later Luke glimpsed both of them outdoors. Oscar was chasing Smits, and Smits had enough of a head start that it might take Oscar a while to catch him.

"What was that all about?" Luke asked.

Mr. Talbot went over to the window, keeping a close eye on the huge man chasing the boy.

"Your brother," he said grimly, "is in danger of being confined to a mental institution."

"A mental institution?" Luke repeated. "Like where they put crazy people? But he's not crazy. A little strange, a little rude—but not crazy."

"He's told people that his older brother, Lee, is dead," Mr. Talbot said, still watching out the window. "Back at his old school he told classmates that his brother was killed by the Government."

Luke gasped. "But—"

Mr. Talbot turned around. "They didn't believe him," he said. "Fortunately, Smits had established quite a reputation as a liar before that. But he is dangerous. In this country a twelve-year-old boy armed with the truth can be very dangerous indeed."

Luke shook his head, trying to make sense of what he'd heard.

"Would the Grants really do that?" Luke asked. "Put

Smits in some insane asylum because he can't keep his mouth shut? They'd send their real son away to—to protect me?"

"The Grants don't care about you," Mr. Talbot said harshly. "They're trying to protect themselves."

Luke shook his head again, but by now he'd given up on anything making sense. If Smits was a liar, how much had he lied to Luke?

"Was Lee Grant really killed by the Government?" Luke asked.

Mr. Talbot looked straight at Luke. He had his eyebrows lowered, his eyes narrowed, his lips pursed. He seemed to be judging what he could and could not safely tell Luke. Finally he said, "Probably."

Oscar and Smits burst back into Mr. Hendricks's house. Oscar had one huge fist gripped around Smits's right arm; Smits was breathing hard but kept glaring resentfully at the man towering over him. When they came to stand at the threshold of the dining room, Luke saw Smits jerk back his leg and give Oscar a sharp kick on the shin. Oscar didn't even flinch.

"I will take Smithfield to his room," Oscar said. "If he cannot show his manners, he does not deserve to eat with civilized people. Lee, you will bring him his homework for the rest of the day."

It was the first time Oscar had ever addressed Luke by name. Was it possible that Oscar still believed the lie?

"Um, sure," Luke said.

And Oscar carried Smits out the door, Smits squirming the whole way.

When they were gone, Luke realized that he finally had what he'd longed for before: Mr. Talbot and Mr. Hendricks to himself. But he was almost too stunned to come up with any more questions. And Mr. Talbot and Mr. Hendricks looked too worried to give him the patient explanations he wanted.

"What do you think will happen to Smits now? And—and to me?" he finally managed to say.

And Mr. Talbot, who always had all the answers, said, "I don't know."

CHAPTER *TEN*

What happened next was—nothing.

Mr. Talbot left and Luke went back to class. He took notes on plant life and musical compositions. Right before dinner he went up to Smits's room to deliver Smits's homework assignments, but Oscar just took them at the door. Luke didn't even catch a glimpse of Smits.

The next day Smits was back in class, as arrogant as ever, with Oscar as menacing as ever standing behind him with his sledgehammer. Just having the two of them there killed all conversation and forced everyone to cast fearful glances over his shoulder, all the time. Luke even caught some of the boys sending resentful stares his way, as if it was his fault that Smits and Oscar were there.

And in some strange way he knew it was. Though he now realized that even Mr. Talbot wasn't sure why the Grants had sent Smits to Hendricks.

A week passed, two weeks, three. Luke kept expecting some dramatic event—maybe another explosion from

Smits. But all he had was math, science, literature. History, music, games. And, every now and then, a summons from Smits after everyone else was asleep.

Smits didn't talk anymore about Lee's death, either as it had really happened or as he pretended it'd happened in a dream. Instead, he'd talk about his memories of Lee, late into the night while Oscar slept—or pretended to sleep.

"Remember that time we played the trick on the butler?" Smits would say. "When he put on his shoes and those firecrackers went off—remember how high he jumped?"

Or, "Remember that nanny who smelled like bananas? And we couldn't figure out why, because she was certainly never allowed to eat any. And then the housekeeper caught her washing her *hair* with banana paste because she'd heard somewhere that that would make it thicker, and she was in love with the chauffeur we had then, and you and I walked in on them once, kissing in the garage. . . ."

Or, "Remember how we kept stealing the maids' feather dusters? You told me they were real birds, and I was scared they'd come to life and fly around the house in the middle of the night. . . ."

Smits's memories didn't always make sense because he'd jump from story to story. And Luke could never tell how old he and Smits were supposed to have been during any of the tales. Had Smits and the real Lee flushed entire rolls of toilet paper down the toilet when they were two and three or when they were eleven and twelve? Luke could hardly ask questions. After all, the stories Smits told were supposed to be Luke's memories, too. He shouldn't need Smits to tell him, for example, how many cooks had gotten seared eyelashes when the flaming dessert exploded at that fancy dinner party their parents had had.

Smits didn't seem to care if Luke understood his ramblings or not. But strangely, after just a few nights, Luke found he could join in the reminiscing, as Smits began to repeat stories Luke had already heard.

"Oh, yeah, the feather dusters!" Luke exclaimed. "I'd almost forgotten about that. Now, why in the world were you so scared of them? You didn't *really* think they could come back to life, did you?"

Smits fixed Luke with a curious look.

"Yes," he said. "I did. I didn't know what death was." And he launched into another tale.

At first Luke only acted—pretending to listen, pretending to care. But slowly he was drawn into Smits's hypnotic unreeling of the lives that he and Lee had once lived. It was all a foreign world to Luke. Luke had grown up on hard work and fear; life for his family had been a constant struggle. Smits and Lee had each had a miniature car they drove around the paths of their estate. Smits had once had a birthday party where an actual circus had come and performed for his thirty-five guests.

But Luke had had a mother who tucked him into bed every night, and a father who would play checkers with him on those dreary winter days when there was no farmwork to be done. Smits and Lee seemed to have had only servants.

One night, at the beginning of Smits's fourth week of storytelling, Luke ventured to ask in the middle of a long, involved tale about a missing teddy bear, "I forget. Where was Mom then?"

Smits stopped and squinted in confusion at Luke.

"I forget, too," he said. "Probably at a party. Entertaining. Like always."

And he went on, telling in outraged terms about the nanny who'd refused to step out onto the roof to retrieve the teddy bear from the rain gutter, where Smits had thrown it.

It wasn't long after that night that Smits said at the very end of a long session of reminiscing, "I'm sorry. I know you've been trying to help. At least you've stayed awake." He rolled his eyes toward the huge, snoring form of Oscar. Luke stifled a yawn of his own and almost missed seeing the stern set of Smits's jaw. Smits looked like a miniature grown-up once again.

"Whatever happens," Smits said, "you can tell people I told you: None of this is because of you. It won't be your fault. I even . . . I even kind of like you."

He sounded surprised.

CHAPTER *ELEVEN*

Luke stumbled back down to his own room, so drowsy that he almost considered just lying down on the stairs and going to sleep there. In the back of his mind he suspected that he needed to figure out exactly what Smits had meant. "Whatever happens . . . it won't be your fault. . . ." But Luke had missed so much sleep staying up with Smits. He felt like his brain was functioning amazingly well just to be able to command his feet: down the stairs, left, right, down, and down again. He knew he wouldn't be capable of thinking about anything important until morning.

And Smits himself was probably already asleep. Whatever Smits thought was going to happen surely wouldn't occur until morning.

Luke reached his room, fell into his bed, and was asleep almost instantly.

Loud, clanging alarms woke him only minutes later, it seemed. He opened his eyes to flashing lights and a voice booming throughout the room: "Evacuate immediately! Evacuate immediately!"

Around him his roommates were sitting up dazedly in their beds, holding their hands over their ears. The voice on the loudspeaker was so intense, Luke could barely think. He saw Trey slip down from the bunk above. Trey's lips were moving, and Luke could tell he was asking Luke a question, but Luke had no hope of hearing Trey over the blaring alarm. Luke gave Trey a confused look and held up his hands helplessly.

Trey leaned in close and screamed directly into Luke's ear: "What if it's a trick? I think we should hide."

Luke shook his head. For the first time something else registered with his brain. He cupped his hand over Trey's ear and yelled as loudly as he could: "No! I smell smoke!"

The loudspeaker voice announced, "You are in danger! The school is on fire! Evacuate immediately! Go through the secret door in your room!"

Secret door? Luke had no idea what that meant. Then suddenly a crack appeared in a blank portion of a wall Luke had never paid much attention to before. Seconds later a door sprang open in the wall, revealing a corridor with dim lights.

Luke looked suspiciously at the door. Trey was worried about tricks—what if the voice was directing them into danger, not away from it? Cautiously Luke stuck his head through the mysterious door. At the end of a dimly lit corridor he could see stairs leading down. Could this be the best way out? He went back to the regular door of his room and jerked on the handle: The door didn't budge. It was locked or stuck. Either way he couldn't open that door. If he and his friends didn't go through the secret door, they'd be trapped.

Luke inhaled sharply. He was sure now. He did smell smoke. The scent was stronger than ever.

"Come on!" Luke yelled, though no one could hear him. He began shoving boys toward the secret door. No one wanted to go. They seemed to prefer to cower in their beds. Luke had to drag Robert across the room, and even then Robert just huddled at the entrance to the secret corridor. Would Luke have to carry him down all those stairs?

Suddenly, out of nowhere, Mr. Dirk, their history teacher, appeared in the doorway to the secret corridor. He grabbed Robert by the arms and pulled him to his feet. Together, Luke and Mr. Dirk shepherded the boys down the steps.

At the bottom Mr. Dirk pressed on a door and it opened, revealing a clear view of the night sky. They were outdoors.

Gratefully Luke gulped in fresh air and rushed out. But around him the other boys balked.

"No!" Luke yelled. "Out!"

Joel and John and Trey slipped fearfully out the door, but Luke had to peel Robert's fingers off the railing of the stairs, had to propel him inch by inch toward the out-doors.

Luke was just ready to step outside himself when Mr. Dirk said into his ear, "Now help me get the rest."

The rest?

In a daze, Luke followed Mr. Dirk back up the stairs. From the secret corridor they entered room after room, pulling boys out of beds and from closets where they were crouched and trembling. Luke lost track of time. He lost track of how many kids he prodded and pulled. Some he even carried. After about the second room he didn't look at faces anymore. He just knew he had to get everyone out.

Finally, finally, Luke and Mr. Dirk reached the bottom of the stairs and Mr. Dirk didn't immediately head back up again. Luke started to—his legs seemed to move on their own.

"No, no," Mr. Dirk said. "Everyone's safe now. We've evacuated everyone on the second and third floors."

He gently pulled Luke back from the stairs. Gratefully Luke finally stepped outside. The cool night air rushed at him. He hadn't realized how sweaty he'd gotten; his pajamas were drenched. His muscles ached. Behind him the alarms didn't seem so blaring, the loudspeaker voice didn't sound so urgent. Everyone was safe now. Everyone from the second and third floor. And nobody would have been on the first floor, because nobody would have been in the classrooms in the middle of the night. As for the fourth floor . . .

Luke whirled around.

"Smits!" he yelled desperately.

CHAPTER *TWELVE*

Luke was ready to race back up the stairs, but Mr. Dirk grabbed his arm.

"The evacuation corridor network doesn't go up to the fourth floor," he said. "I'm sure Smits got out by other means. He doesn't have the same, uh, fears as the rest of you boys."

Frantically Luke looked up, toward the top of the school. He wanted so badly to see a gaping hole made by Oscar's precious sledgehammer. Instead, he saw only smooth brick, all the way to the roof, seemingly unmarred by either fire or escape. A few last tendrils of smoke rose toward the moon.

"Looks like the fire's out," Mr. Dirk said cheerfully. "I'm not sure how serious it was to begin with, but it's good we had such a successful test of our evacuation procedure. It was my idea, you know. We figured you boys would naturally be inclined to want to hide in an emergency, so we thought we'd have to work around that tendency. Don't you think the secret doors and corridors and stairs worked great?"

Luke had never heard Mr. Dirk talk so much about any event that hadn't happened centuries ago.

"You were a wonderful help, I must say," Mr. Dirk rambled on.

"I have to find Smits," Luke said rudely, and walked away.

All the other boys were standing or sitting numbly in clusters around the yard. Luke went from group to group, asking again and again, "Have you seen Smits? Have you seen Smits?"

Nobody had.

Even in his desperate search for Smits, Luke couldn't help but notice how stricken all his friends and classmates were. Luke wasn't sure if they were traumatized by being pulled from their beds in the middle of the night because of a fire—or if they were simply terrified of being outdoors. But several of the boys were shaking uncontrollably. Some were even crying.

"There, there, everything's okay," someone said soothingly.

Luke turned around. It was Mr. Hendricks. He had rolled his wheelchair across the rough lawn and was patting one of the younger boys on the back. Luke rushed to his side.

"Is everyone safe?" Luke demanded. "Is Smits?"

Mr. Hendricks gave Luke a measuring look.

"Yes, everyone's safe," he said. "Smits and Oscar are at my house right now, locked in separate rooms."

"Why?" Luke asked, bewildered.

"Smits is accusing Oscar of setting the fire, of trying to kill him," Mr. Hendricks said. "And Oscar is accusing Smits."

CHAPTER *THIRTEEN*

Luke wanted to ask questions; he wanted Mr. Hendricks to solve every mystery right then and there. But Mr. Hendricks was already turning to other boys, repeating again and again, "It's all right. You're safe."

"They need to be indoors," Luke muttered. He looked around at the forlorn clusters of boys scattered across the shadowy lawn. "Is there room for everyone in your house, Mr. Hendricks?"

"An excellent idea," Mr. Hendricks said. He raised his voice. "Hot apple cider and biscuits will be served at the headmaster's house in five minutes."

Fearfully the boys began moving through the darkness. Once again Luke got stuck herding the others.

"It's safe on the path, really," he had to assure one boy after another. "You're not going anywhere dangerous."

He had thought his classmates had made so much progress, had become so much braver. All that seemed to have been erased tonight.

Once everyone got to Mr. Hendricks's house, they all crowded in eagerly. Nobody wanted to be left out on the porch, even if it meant standing shoulder to shoulder, elbow to elbow. Someone started a brigade of biscuits and cups of cider. The cider sloshed on the floor and crumbs dropped everywhere, but no one seemed to care. They were all coming back to life.

"When that door opened in my room, I couldn't believe my eyes," Joel said.

"Did anybody know those doors were there?" John asked.

"Why didn't they just let us go out the regular doors?" Robert asked.

"Because they knew we'd all be too scared," Trey said glumly. "They knew we were cowards."

Trey seemed thoroughly disgusted with himself. He wouldn't meet Luke's eyes. Luke thought about how he'd feel now if he'd been one of the boys cowering in their beds or trembling in their closets. He felt a surge of pride; he, at least, had been brave. This time.

"Hey, maybe there wasn't a fire at all. Maybe this was just a drill," Joel said. "Maybe it was just a test Luke and the teachers cooked up to see how we'd react. They probably got the idea from Smits, talking about needing a sledgehammer to escape."

He and several other boys turned almost accusingly toward Luke.

"No, there was a fire," Trey said dully. "Didn't you smell the smoke?"

"Hey, where is Smits?" John asked. "Why isn't he here bragging about how *his* bodyguard got him out, because he's so rich and *his* life is so much more valuable than any of ours?"

Now everyone looked expectantly toward Luke, waiting for him to explain. Smits wasn't even Luke's real brother, and Luke was still supposed to be Smits's keeper.

"He's here in Mr. Hendricks's house, too," Luke said. "He's just in a different room."

"*He's* probably got a room to himself," Joel said resentfully.

Luke didn't answer this time. He was still trying to make sense of what Mr. Hendricks had told him. The last thing he wanted to do was try to explain everything to the others, who didn't think much of Smits anyway. But they didn't like Oscar, either. They'd probably want to blame both of them for setting the fire.

Luke was pretty sure he knew which one was guilty. But why?

The conversation seemed to swirl away from Luke as the other boys moved from the dining room to the kitchen. Only Trey stayed by Luke's side.

"Weren't you scared at all?" Trey asked softly. "Why didn't you want to hide, too?"

Luke thought back. It was hard to remember what he had been thinking when that first alarm went off, when that first order came over the loudspeaker: "Evacuate immediately!" He wasn't even sure if he had been thinking.

"I probably did want to hide," he told Trey. "I just knew that I couldn't. And I was worried about everyone else."

"Of course," Trey said. "That's because you're brave. You're a hero. And I'm not. I never will be."

Luke remembered how miserable he'd been when he found out that his friend Jen had died at the rally for third children's rights, when Luke hadn't even had the courage to go to it. But Luke, at least, had had the comfort of knowing that his cowardice—if that's what it was—had probably saved his life. Trey's cowardice could have led to his death.

"I'll make you a deal," Luke said lightly. "Next time, you're welcome to be the hero instead of me."

Trey shook his head. "I'm not joking," he said. "It's not that easy. When I'm terrified, I can't just stand up and say, 'Well, it's hero time!' I can't. And you—you went back into a burning building, what—six, seven, eight times? You risked your life."

Luke didn't like thinking about what he had done in those terms.

"There wasn't that much danger," Luke said. "I never even saw any flames."

"That's because the escape corridors are sealed," Trey said. "Mr. Dirk explained everything. They sealed off our dormitory rooms and the escape route as soon as the first alarm went off. It really is an ingenious system. None of us deserve it. Except you."

Luke had never seen Trey like this before. Trey had never

seemed to mind being easily frightened; he'd never seemed to long for courage. What had the fire done to him?

"All right, everyone," Mr. Hendricks announced at the front of the room. "We've now checked the entire school thoroughly. It's safe for all of you to go back to your rooms. I realize this has been a disruptive experience—all morning classes are canceled, so you all may sleep late."

The boys had recovered enough of their spirit that they managed to raise a feeble cheer. But the exuberance died as soon as they began moving out into the darkness once more, facing their fears of the outdoors yet again.

Luke moved around the edges of the crowd, thinking he'd need to guide the others along the path to the school. But Mr. Hendricks stopped him at the door.

"Not you," he said, laying a cautioning hand on Luke's arm. "I need your help."

"With Smits?" Luke asked.

Mr. Hendricks nodded. "And Oscar."

CHAPTER *FOURTEEN*

Luke waited on the couch until all the other boys were gone. When Mr. Hendricks finally shut the front door and rolled his wheelchair back toward Luke, Luke started to blurt out, "Mr. Hendricks, it had to have been Smits who set the fire. He told me—"

Mr. Hendricks held up his hand, stopping Luke.

"Now, now," he said. "The last thing I need right now is to hear any more wild accusations. Think very carefully before you tell me anything."

What would it hurt to tell Mr. Hendricks the truth? Luke wondered. He slumped on the couch in confusion.

"One of the few things that Oscar and Smits agree on is that you were the last one in Smits's room last evening," Mr. Hendricks said. "Besides the two of them, of course. What I would like you to do for me right now is to go up to Smits's room and tell me if you see anything amiss. Apart from the fire damage, that is."

"The fire was in Smits's room?" Luke asked.

Mr. Hendricks nodded.

"Entirely," he said. "We were able to contain it quite successfully."

Luke's certainty ebbed a bit. No matter what Smits had said, why would Smits want to burn his own room?

But for that matter, why would Oscar want to injure the boy he was supposed to be protecting?

Luke could easily understand why Mr. Hendricks looked so troubled. Luke stood up.

"All right," he said. "I'll be back in a few minutes."

He went out the front door. The night air that had felt like such a relief only an hour or so ago seemed cold now. Threatening. Luke felt like he'd caught the other boys' fear.

But none of the other boys were going to have to inspect a charred room all by themselves. Only Luke.

In his head Luke carried on an imaginary conversation with Mr. Hendricks and Mr. Talbot: *Guess what? When I said I was willing to be brave for the cause of helping to free all the third children, this isn't what I meant. This is scaring me—this is danger, for no reason. This has nothing to do with the cause. Smits isn't my concern. Smits shouldn't be my problem.*

But he couldn't imagine what Mr. Hendricks's or Mr. Talbot's response would be if he actually spoke those words to either of them.

Luke slipped in the front door of the school and lightly raced up the stairs. He saw none of the other boys, but some of the teachers seemed to be patrolling the halls. No one stopped Luke.

On the fourth floor the smell of smoke was overpowering. Luke longed for an open window to lean his head out. But except for the smell, Luke found no other evidence of fire until he reached the door of Smits's room. The door was pulled shut, but burn marks spiked out from the frame. Gently Luke pushed the door open.

The room he'd stood in only hours before was transformed. The carpet was covered with wet ash; the comforter on the bed was burned away. Luke thought about what little Mr. Hendricks had told him about Oscar's and Smits's differing versions of how the fire had started. Could Oscar possibly have set Smits's bed on fire while Smits was in it?

To still the terrifying questions growing in his mind, Luke moved over to Smits's desk, which seemed relatively untouched. His schoolbooks were stacked neatly off to the side, only slightly charred but, like much of the rest of the room, soaking wet. The computer everyone had been so impressed by when Smits arrived was now only a sad heap of melted plastic.

Luke wanted to run away, to rush back to Mr. Hendricks and report, "I didn't see anything strange." And then maybe he could wiggle out of any obligation Mr. Hendricks thought he had to Smits and Oscar; he could go back to bed like all the other boys. He could fall asleep and tell himself that everything frightening him was just a nightmare.

But something made Luke keep looking, methodically,

with a sort of horrified fascination. He pulled out drawers, examined papers that had managed to escape all flame. But they were just ordinary homework—musical scales and conjugated verbs. Luke moved away from the desk. In the closet, totally unscathed, he found the folded-up cot that Oscar evidently slept on when he wasn't sleeping in the chair.

And then, tucked under the sheet, inside a split seam of the cot's mattress, Luke found something rigid and plastic and rectangular. Luke dug into the mattress and pulled out two identification cards.

Fake ones.

Or were they?

CHAPTER *FIFTEEN*

One of the I.D. cards showed Smits's face but a different name: Peter Goodard. The other I.D. showed no picture, just a name: Stanley Goodard. Why was the picture missing? Had the fire prevented Oscar from gluing his picture on—or from taking Smits's picture off? Were Oscar and Smits really not Oscar and Smits, but Peter and Stanley? Or were they really Oscar and Smits, planning to go undercover as other people? Why would they want to do that? And whose plan was it? Oscar/Stanley's or Smits/Peter's?

Luke felt so overwhelmed that he sank to the floor, neither remembering nor caring that he'd get ash all over his clothes. He stared at the fake I.D.'s in his trembling hands.

"Are you finding everything satisfactorily?" a voice said behind him, from the doorway of the room. It was Mr. Dirk.

Luke scrambled to hide the I.D.'s. He slid his hand toward his pant pocket, forgetting he was still wearing pajamas. And even fancy Baron pajamas lacked pockets in the pants. The only pocket was on the pajama shirt.

Desperately he cupped the I.D.'s in his hand, trying to keep them out of sight.

"Mr. Hendricks sent me to check on you because you were taking so long," Mr. Dirk said.

"Oh—I was just being thorough," Luke said. "Like you tell us to be on essay tests."

Mr. Dirk laughed, without any humor.

Would there be any harm in telling Mr. Dirk the secret Luke had just discovered? Luke certainly intended to tell Mr. Hendricks, and Mr. Hendricks trusted Mr. Dirk. Then Luke remembered what Mr. Hendricks had said: "Think very carefully before you tell me anything." What was Mr. Hendricks so afraid of? Shouldn't Luke pass the burden of this secret to a trustworthy grown-up as soon as possible?

He wanted to. But something made him keep quiet.

"So, thorough or not—are you almost done? Mr. Hendricks is waiting, you know," Mr. Dirk said.

"Um, sure," Luke said.

He turned slowly, trying to slip the I.D. cards up his sleeve as he moved. And because he stayed low to the floor, for the first time he saw what lay under Smits's bed.

"Oscar's sledgehammer," Luke said, and pointed with the hand that wasn't hiding the I.D. cards.

Mr. Dirk walked into the room, his shoes squishing on the wet, burned carpet. He bent down and pulled the sledgehammer out from under the bed. It was near the head of the bed, directly below the pillows that Smits had been lying on the last time Luke had seen him.

"Is that a clue?" Luke asked. "Is it important where we found it?"

"Perhaps," Mr. Dirk said. "I'm not a forensics expert. This is why I like history. With the advantage of hindsight you can almost always tell what's important."

Luke tried to remember whether Oscar had been holding the sledgehammer the last time Luke had been in Smits's room. But Luke hadn't been paying attention to Oscar then.

"I'll take it to Mr. Hendricks," Luke said. "He'll know what to do with it."

Grasping the sledgehammer in one hand and holding the I.D.'s inside his pajama sleeve with the other, Luke left Mr. Dirk looking perplexed, standing in the middle of Smits's ruined room.

Back at Mr. Hendricks's house, Luke silently laid the sledgehammer and the two I.D.'s on the dining-room table. Mr. Hendricks's eyes widened in surprise when he saw the I.D.'s, but he quickly swept them from the table and thrust them back at Luke.

"Keep these out of sight," he said. "Did anyone else see them?"

Luke was relieved that he could shake his head no. Still, he carefully slipped the I.D.'s into the pocket of the pajama shirt.

"This is an interesting development indeed," Mr. Hendricks muttered, seemingly to himself.

"What if this is who Smits and Oscar really are?" Luke asked, tapping the pocket. "What if they've been lying about their identities all along?"

"Smits is Smits, all right," Mr. Hendricks said. "I've no doubt of that. But Oscar could be anyone. That's why he's dangerous."

Luke shook his head, trying to clear it. Outside Mr. Hendricks's windows Luke could see the first tinge of dawn creeping over the horizon. And Luke had had barely five minutes of sleep all night. That must be the reason it took so long for Mr. Hendricks's words to register. When they did, he jumped back in panic.

"Oscar could be anyone?" he repeated. "Do you think he's from the Population Police?"

"No," Mr. Hendricks said, "but you might want to act as though he is."

Luke squinted at Mr. Hendricks in total confusion. Mr. Hendricks sighed and handed Luke a set of keys.

"Smits is in the back bedroom," he said. "Why don't you go get him and bring him to me?"

Luke half expected Smits to be asleep, but he sprang out of the room the instant Luke got the door open.

"Am I safe now? Have you sent that murdering scum off to jail where he belongs?" Smits yelled. Then he slumped against the doorframe as soon as he saw it was only Luke. "Oh, Lee. Hi."

"Are you out of your mind?" Luke asked.

The younger boy didn't answer, only followed Luke down the hall. When they reached the dining room and he saw the sledgehammer lying on the table, Smits resumed his hysteria.

"So you found Oscar's weapon," Smits raged. "Under the bed, right? He never meant to use that to save me, you know. I'm lucky he never bludgeoned me to death in my sleep."

"Smits," Mr. Hendricks said patiently, "how did you know where Oscar hid the sledgehammer, to avoid saving you, if, as you told me before, you were asleep when he supposedly set the fire?"

Smits visibly wilted.

Mr. Hendricks shook his head. "Smits, with as many untruths as you've been accused of telling, I'd think you'd be a more accomplished liar by now."

"That's my problem," Smits said sulkily. "I've never been a good liar. Haven't you ever noticed? The people who are good at it never get caught. If I could lie well, I wouldn't be here right now."

Luke wondered exactly what Smits meant by that.

"Smits," Mr. Hendricks said gently, "why did you set the fire?"

Smits looked down. "I wanted you to send Oscar away," he mumbled. Then he peered earnestly at Mr. Hendricks. "Couldn't you still do that? Couldn't you tell my parents that he was to blame, and then they'd fire him and he'd go away? And you could tell them that I'm doing really well here, so I don't need another bodyguard. . . ."

"And what would that accomplish?" Mr. Hendricks asked.

Smits looked from Mr. Hendricks to Luke.

"Then I could act the way I want to act. I wouldn't be . . . spied on. I could find out . . ." He broke off and looked back at the floor.

"Find out what?" Mr. Hendricks asked.

But Smits only shook his head. He kept his face down. Luke wondered if he'd started crying.

"Sit down, Smits," Mr. Hendricks said. "Lee, could you go open Oscar's door now?"

So Luke took another key and went to another door at the back of the house. Like Smits, Oscar was waiting close to the door. But when Oscar saw Luke, he said nothing, only rushed past him, out to Mr. Hendricks.

"I must call my employers," Oscar announced. "I demand to be given a phone this instant!"

Mr. Hendricks gave Oscar an amused look.

"I believe, as headmaster of this school, that I shall be the one calling the Grants," he said. "If they ask to speak to you, I shall, of course, let them. Now, sit!"

Oscar sat. Luke hid a smile at the sight of the huge, muscular man obeying the command of an old man in a wheelchair. Oscar could easily have overpowered Mr. Hendricks and grabbed as many phones as he wanted. But Mr. Hendricks had such an aura of control about him, Luke bet that it didn't even occur to Oscar to disobey.

Mr. Hendricks rolled into his office to use the phone. Oscar, Luke, and Smits sat silently around the dining-room table. After a few moments Oscar reached out and grabbed his sledgehammer. Luke saw Smits flinch beside him. But Oscar didn't do anything with the hammer, only cradled it in his arms.

Then Mr. Hendricks returned.

"The Grants have been informed now that we had a minor fire at our school, possibly electrical in nature," he said. He looked directly at Smits. "They want you to come home as soon as possible, until our wiring can be thoroughly checked. For safety's sake."

"But—," Smits protested.

Luke noticed that Oscar looked ready to complain, too, but he kept his mouth shut.

"They were adamant," Mr. Hendricks said. "I don't believe that anything you might say would change their minds. Now, why don't you and Oscar go and pack up whatever can be salvaged from your room?"

Astonished, Luke watched Smits and his bodyguard leave.

"You trust the two of them alone together?" Luke asked as soon as they were out the door.

"Yes," Mr. Hendricks said. "As long as Oscar stays awake. And I don't believe he'll be sleeping anytime soon."

The notion of sleep sounded mighty good to Luke. But he still had one more question before he left, too.

"Why didn't you tell the Grants the truth about how the fire started?" Luke asked.

"In a country as full of lies as ours," Mr. Hendricks said, "sometimes the truth doesn't matter as much as what people like the Grants believe."

Luke frowned, trying to understand. "You're giving Smits another chance," he said.

Mr. Hendricks nodded. "You could look at it that way. Though I'm not sure how much of a chance I've given him.

I'm sure Oscar will be eager to tell them his version of events. Anyway, as you're always reminding me, the phone lines aren't secure. No need to alert any eavesdroppers to problems here."

Luke shrugged. What Mr. Hendricks said made sense. It occurred to Luke that with Smits and Oscar leaving, all his problems were over. He just couldn't imagine Smits ever returning, not if his parents found out the truth. Luke wouldn't even need to worry about the mystery of the fake I.D.'s now. He could have his old life back. He and his friends could talk about being shadow children again. They wouldn't have to pretend for the sake of the spoiled rich kid and the hulking bodyguard in their midst.

Luke felt like a massive burden had just been lifted from his shoulders. He turned to go, certain that, for the first time in more than a month, he'd finally get some good sleep.

"Luke," Mr. Hendricks said behind him. "The Grants didn't want just Smits and Oscar to come home."

"Huh?" Luke said.

"They're worried about the safety of both their sons."

Luke whirled around. "You don't mean—"

"Yes, Luke," Mr. Hendricks said. "When the chauffeur returns to pick up Smits tomorrow, they want him to bring you home, too."

CHAPTER *SIXTEEN*

Luke gaped at Mr. Hendricks.

"You told them no, didn't you? You told them I was fine here, right?" he said.

Mr. Hendricks sighed. "Luke, your father is a very powerful man. Some would say he has as much control over our country as the president. Nobody tells him no."

"But—"

"And, legally, you are his son. You're underage. He can order you to go anywhere he wants."

Luke was practically shaking now. He fought to keep his fears under control.

"What do they want from me?" he asked.

Mr. Hendricks grimaced.

"I don't know," he said. "I'm sorry. I really wish I did. There's something going on here that I don't understand. The best thing I can do is get Smits and Oscar away from my school. I have to protect my students."

Now Luke wondered whose idea it had been to send Smits and Oscar home.

"*I'm* one of your students, too," he said. "Don't you want to protect me?" He didn't wait for an answer. "I know. Why don't you call Mr. Talbot, have him come and give me a different fake I.D. I'm not Lee Grant. I don't have to be. Let me be somebody else. Somebody who can stay here."

But Mr. Hendricks was shaking his head. "Don't you know how hard it was to get this identity for you? Don't you know how many kids are still in hiding, still waiting for what you already have?"

Luke squirmed, trying to avoid Mr. Hendricks's gaze. The fake I.D.'s in his shirt pocket poked his chest, giving him an idea.

"What about one of these identities?" he asked, tapping the pocket. "I could be Peter or Stanley. I've got my choice."

"Do you really think it could be that easy?" Mr. Hendricks asked. "You've got no idea what baggage those identities carry. What if the real Stanley Goodard, who-ever he is, is wanted for murder? What if—"

"Okay, okay. I get the point," Luke grumbled.

Mr. Hendricks's expression softened. "I'm sorry. But you can't swap identities just like that. Even if it were easy to fake being someone else, you can't cast off Lee Grant. Not now. Because, for some reason, *they* want you to be Lee now."

Luke remembered what Smits had said to him on

Smits's first night at Hendricks: "Can you be Lee?" Why would Smits or his parents care?

And did they care for the same reasons?

Luke couldn't sort out his feelings. What did he really think would happen to him at the Grants'? He didn't know. That was the problem.

Luke thought about what Trey had said to him barely an hour ago: "You're a hero. . . ." Trey thought Luke was so brave. Luke wanted Mr. Hendricks to think that, too. Luke wished he could pull off an unconcerned act, could shrug casually and say something like, "Well, if I've got to go, I've got to go. If Mr. Grant's so powerful, how about if I talk him into freeing all the third children while I'm there?" But Luke wasn't brave. He was terrified. Rushing into a burning building and convincing cowering boys to leave seemed like nothing compared with going to the Grants' house with Smits and Oscar.

A new thought occurred to him.

"The servants will know I'm not really Lee," he said. "Mr. and Mrs. Grant's friends will see me. . . ."

"The Grants don't seem worried about that," Mr. Hendricks said. "We'll have to have faith that that won't be a problem."

Luke bit his lip, trying to think of another obstacle.

"Luke, I don't know if this helps, but . . . I do wish I could protect you, too," Mr. Hendricks said gently. "I just can't. But I will tell you—of all the boys at Hendricks, you're the one I'd trust the most to come out of this safely.

Just use your common sense. You'll be all right."

And so those were the words Luke repeated to himself, over and over again, a mere two hours later as he climbed into a limousine behind Smits to go to a home that wasn't his.

You'll be all right, you'll be all right, you'll be all right. . . .

Luke just wished he could believe it.

CHAPTER *SEVENTEEN*

Did you notice, Lee? It's a new chauffeur," Smits said after he pulled a panel of glass shut between the driver and the space where he, Oscar, and Luke reclined on luxurious leather seats. Luke thought Hendricks School was formal and fancy, but just the interior of this car made Hendricks look like a hovel. Luke had a feeling he'd better get over being awestruck right now—the Grants' house was likely to be even more ostentatious.

He wasn't sure how to deal with Smits, so he only shrugged and kept looking out the window. They had driven past Mr. Hendricks's cottage already; they were turning out onto the main road.

"Our parents never keep servants for very long," Smits continued.

Was Smits trying to tell Luke something? Like, maybe Luke would be safe at the Grants', since there would be no old servants to remember what the real Lee had looked like?

No, Smits was talking to Oscar now.

"Did you hear me?" he demanded. "I said our parents never keep servants around for very long. They must have fired the last chauffeur. And as soon as they hear what happened at Hendricks, they'll fire you, too."

"Smits, the last chauffeur was fired because of you," Oscar said. "He was fired because you bribed him into tricking me."

"So?" Smits taunted. "And you'll be dismissed because of me, too. Because you didn't protect me during the fire."

"You set it yourself!" Oscar roared.

Smits gave a so-what shrug. For once Luke could sympathize with Oscar's rage. Whenever he closed his eyes, Luke could still see the fear in the faces of his friends—friends he hadn't even had a chance to say good-bye to.

"Smits, lots of other boys could have died because of you," Luke said. "That fire could have burned down the whole school."

"Aw, there were sprinklers in every room," Smits said. "There wasn't any danger."

Was that true? Had Luke's heroism been for little more than a fire drill? Strangely, he felt as though Smits had taken something away from him.

Luke turned his face back to the window, hoping Smits would get the message that he wasn't in the mood to talk. The limousine was driving down a road Luke had never seen before—which wasn't terribly surprising. Luke had been in a car only once before, when Mr. Talbot had driven him from his family's farm to Hendricks School. Luke had felt so overwhelmed then, he'd barely been able to take in anything he saw. Now he forced himself to pay attention. What kind of people lived in those tiny houses by the road? Was anyone tending the derelict fields? It was nearly October now—why wasn't the countryside full of farmers busy with harvest? Luke was sure that, back home, his father and brothers were working frantically. His mother had probably taken time off from the chicken factory to help out. Did they still miss Luke as much as he missed them?

Luke swallowed a lump in his throat and closed his eyes. Sometimes it was better not to pay attention. It would be better not to think about where he was going, either, or what he might face there. . . .

The next thing Luke knew, the car had stopped and the chauffeur was peering in through the open door.

"Please, sirs," he said timidly. "Please? You are home now, no? Your parents will be wanting me to help you out. Sirs?"

Groggily Luke forced himself to open his eyes. He had been so soundly asleep that for a long moment he had trouble remembering where he was. Why wasn't he in his bed at Hendricks, staring up at the bottom of Trey's bunk? Why was his face stuck to his pillow? Or no, it wasn't his pillow. Why was he sleeping on a leather seat?

Outdoors, behind the chauffeur, Luke could see what looked like thousands of diamonds hanging from the sky.

Even when Luke peeled his face away from the seat and shook his head to clear his mind a little, the diamonds didn't disappear. Except now he could tell that they were cascading from a roof covering the driveway.

The chauffeur saw where Luke was looking.

"You like your mother's new chandelier, no?" he said. "That is new since you were home last, no?"

And Luke didn't know how to answer. Already an innocent question had stumped him.

On the opposite seat Smits and Oscar were also waking and stretching. Smits scowled at the chauffeur.

"It's ugly, you idiot," Smits said. "That's the ugliest chandelier we've ever had."

Sure, Smits was rude. But at least he'd saved Luke from having to answer.

Dazed, Luke stepped out of the car onto a driveway that was paved with thousands of tiny tiles, all intricately connected. Above him the chandelier swayed in the breeze. Luke stared at it in disbelief. A huge gold globe hung from the portico, with bars reaching out to a dozen smaller globes, all in a circle. The diamonds dangled in ropes from each of the smaller globes, twisting together and coming to a point in a huge crystal directly beneath the largest gold globe. Each of the diamonds threw out rainbows of light all over the portico. Really, Luke decided, the chandelier couldn't be diamonds; there couldn't be that many huge diamonds in the whole world. The chandelier was probably just glass, and Luke couldn't tell the difference.

Either way, it was breathtaking, stunning beyond words.

Everything was. The walls of the Grant mansion rose before him like a sheer cliff; he really couldn't tell where the mansion ended and the rest of the world began. Luke wouldn't have been terribly surprised if the mansion *didn't* end. Unlike Hendricks School, the Grant mansion had windows, dozens and dozens of them, all split into intricate panes of heavy leaded glass. Each pane of each window shone as though the glass was polished on an hourly basis. For all Luke knew, maybe it was.

On the other side of the limousine a velvet green yard stretched out to a row of perfectly trimmed trees. Luke could see no other houses in any direction. The Grants' estate seemed every bit as secluded as Luke's family's farm had been.

"You missed your home?" the chauffeur said to Luke. "You are glad to be home now, no?"

Imitating Smits's rudeness, Luke only shrugged this time.

"Oh, oh, allow me to announce you," the chauffeur said.

He stepped up to the double front doors and threw them open.

"Your sons are home!" he said, his voice taking on a regal rumble.

Smits stepped over the threshold first, onto a gleaming white floor. Luke hesitantly followed him.

"They're probably not even home," Smits said bitterly. "Dad's at work. And Mom's at a party, of course."

But footsteps were coming down the long, curving hallway. Just from the way they sounded—authoritative, commanding—Luke could tell it wasn't servants headed toward him. A man and a woman came into sight. They were probably as old as or older than Luke's parents, but their faces didn't have lines and sags like Luke's father's, their eyes didn't look frightened and defeated like Luke's mother's. The woman had blond hair, styled into a helmet of perfect curls. She wore a brilliant red sweater and dark pants. The man had dark hair, dark eyes, and a dark suit. Luke didn't need to see any price tags to know that everything they wore was very, very expensive. He decided the couple didn't look the least bit like parents. Luke couldn't imagine either one of them bandaging a scraped knee, burping a crying baby, kissing a child's forehead. Of course, if Smits's stories about all the servants were true, they probably never had.

"My boys!" the woman shrieked in a dignified kind of way. "We've been counting the minutes until you got home!"

Luke braced himself to be ignored. He'd have to act normal, somehow, for the sake of the servants—the chauffeur and what looked like three maids peeking in from a nearby room. Luke just wasn't sure what passed for normal behavior in a house like this. He watched Smits for clues, but Smits had gone all stiff, waiting for his parents to finish rushing down the hall.

And then Mrs. Grant brushed right past Smits and

grabbed up Luke in a dizzying embrace. Luke got a whiff of elegant perfume, and then she released him. She stood back, looking him up and down.

"Oh, Lee, you have grown so much while you were away," she exclaimed. "Why, last fall you barely came up to my shoulder. And now . . ." Now Luke could look her straight in the face, eyeball to eyeball, if only he had the nerve. "Oh, I've missed you! Why did you have to stay away for a whole year?"

She wrapped him in another hug. Over her shoulder Luke caught a glimpse of Smits's face. His whole expression had crumpled in pain.

"Smits," Mr. Grant said, quite formally, and offered his son a hand to shake.

Luke expected the two parents to trade off—with Mrs. Grant hugging Smits and Mr. Grant thrusting a stiff hand at Luke. But when Mrs. Grant released Luke a second time, the two grown-ups only stood there, staring awkwardly at the two boys. Smits made no move toward his mother, and he might as well have been invisible, for all the attention she paid him. At least Mr. Grant managed a curt nod toward Luke.

"Well, you'll want to get settled in your rooms," Mrs. Grant said at last. "You must be tired after your journey. Oscar, could you . . ."

Mrs. Grant didn't even have to finish her request. Oscar stepped forward, practically standing on Smits's heels.

"I'm going, I'm going," Smits muttered.

Luke felt like saying, "Don't you want to know what happened at school? Don't you know that those two are dangerous together?" He was used to his own parents, who would have been curious. Who would have been concerned.

He watched Smits step past his mother. She barely flickered her eyes in his direction. Her lips flattened into a thin line of disapproval. From the side Luke could see the emotions playing over Smits's face: first pain, then fury.

Smits had wanted his mother to hug him, too.

Luke didn't understand what he'd witnessed, or why he'd been hugged in Smits's stead. He still didn't understand why the Grants wanted him there. But he could tell that he'd just been sent to his room.

And he didn't have the slightest clue where it was.

CHAPTER *EIGHTEEN*

The chauffeur saved him. He came in just then carrying the luggage, and Luke simply followed him. Up the stairs, down a long, stately hall. Up more stairs, just a half flight, into an entirely different wing of the house. Finally, when Luke was sure he'd walked more than a mile, the chauffeur deposited Luke's luggage and Smits's luggage in adjoining rooms.

Luke hesitated in the doorway of what must have been Lee's room. He looked back at Smits and Oscar, who were still lingering in the hall.

"Just leave me alone!" Smits snarled. "I'm home now! I'm safe! Okay?"

"You think there is not danger here?" Oscar replied. "You think I believe that *you* are not dangerous here?"

Luke slipped into Lee's room, hoping the other two hadn't noticed him listening. And then, staring, he forgot everything else.

The whole rest of the house was luxurious and elegant

beyond belief. But Lee's room was the first place that looked fun. At one end of the room four couches were clustered around a large-screen TV. An entire video arcade lurked in a nearby alcove. Another alcove looked like a sporting goods store: Skis, golf clubs, hockey sticks, tennis rackets, and entire barrels of footballs, baseballs, and basketballs were arranged artfully in every corner. A third alcove held a set of drums and three guitars.

"You play?" the chauffeur asked. Luke had totally forgotten about him. But he was staring longingly at the guitars.

"Some," Luke lied, figuring that the real Lee must have. He hoped the chauffeur wouldn't ask for a demonstration.

But the chauffeur only nodded and bowed, and walked out.

Luke wandered around the room for a while, feeling lost. He looked into drawers of neatly folded clothes. He pulled out a pair of pants and held them up against his own waist. The pant legs ended about the same place as the pants he was actually wearing, but he wasn't sure what that proved. Had the real Lee been about the same height as Luke, or had the Grants secretly found out what size clothes Luke wore, and stocked the room accordingly?

Luke was really looking for something personal—some proof that a real boy had lived here. Initials carved in the bed frame, maybe, or an old drawing of an airplane that Mrs. Grant (or the nanny?) had deemed too special to be thrown out. Luke would even have settled for some signs of wear on the basketballs. But everything looked new and unused. If this had truly been the real Lee's room, he'd passed through this place without leaving behind so much as a smudge on the wall.

Or all signs of his presence had been erased.

Luke shivered at that thought. Suddenly spooked, he went next door to Smits's room, which was every bit as expansive as Lee's.

Smits was sprawled across the bed, staring up at the ceiling. Oscar was nowhere in sight.

"Smits, can you tell me . . ." Luke began.

Smits shook his head and put his finger over his lips. He pointed over to an open door, where Luke could see a figure in a black dress bent over a porcelain sink. A maid was cleaning the bathroom.

"Oh, yeah, it's great to be home," Smits said. "Home, where even the walls have ears."

"I just wondered if you wanted to go down with me and get a snack," Luke finished lamely.

The maid came out of the bathroom.

"Now, don't you boys be ruining your appetites," she scolded. "The cooks have been working all day on a fancy welcome-home dinner for you."

Nothing could have ruined Luke's appetite. Breakfast back at Hendricks School had been heartier than usual, but that had been hours ago. Still, if Smits didn't go with him, he wasn't sure he could find the kitchen. And without Smits he wouldn't have the nerve to rummage through it, looking for food.

"I'm not hungry anyway," Smits said.

Luke's stomach growled. He tried to ignore it. "Want to go outside and play, then? Shoot some hoops or something?"

"Nah," Smits said. "Outside the trees have ears."

There were gardeners, Luke guessed. He supposed that Smits was trying to warn him. He supposed that he ought to be grateful.

But what Luke really wanted to do was punch Smits right smack in the nose. It was almost as bad as if Smits really were his brother.

CHAPTER *NINETEEN*

T he rest of the day felt interminable. Luke wandered aimlessly around the house and grounds for several hours. He didn't encounter either of Smits's parents again, but there seemed to be a servant around every corner. And they all seemed to know everything about him—or, at least, about the person he was supposed to be.

"Have you brought up those grades in mathematics, Master Lee?" a man Luke guessed was a butler asked him in the front hallway.

"I tuned up the engine on your motor scooter, sir," a mechanic in a grease-covered uniform told him out beside the garage, which looked large enough to hold a boat—and probably did, come to think of it.

As the grandfather clock by the front door chimed seven, a housekeeper scolded him, "There you are! Why aren't you washed up and dressed for dinner?"

"I . . . ," Luke protested. He scrambled toward what he thought was the dining room. He remembered seeing a

MARGARET PETERSON HADDIX

vast wooden table in one of these rooms—now, where was it?

Mostly by luck Luke arrived in the proper room. Mr. and Mrs. Grant were seated at opposite ends of the huge table. Two chairs were arranged between them. Smits sat in one of those chairs. Luke dashed toward the other one.

"And where is your tuxedo, young man?" Mrs. Grant asked.

"Um . . . ," Luke said. He noticed that both Smits and Mr. Grant were in formal black suits, with pure white shirts underneath and black bows tied crisply around their necks.

"We didn't dress for dinner at school," Smits volunteered. "Lee probably forgot all about it."

"Indeed," Mrs. Grant sniffed. "Well, we shan't have you forgetting here. Go and change this instant."

Luke considered himself quite fortunate to be able to find his way back to his room, find a suit—a tuxedo?—in his closet, and scramble into it. He was fumbling with the tie, wondering how angry the Grants would be if he just forgot about it—versus how angry they'd be if he kept them waiting any longer—when Oscar silently stepped into the room and adeptly twisted the tie into shape. He straightened the sleeves of Luke's coat, shoved a stray lock of hair off Luke's forehead, and pushed him out the door without saying a single word.

Back in the dining room Mrs. Grant purred, "Now, that's better. That's the son I like to see." Then she, Mr.

Grant, and Smits began spooning up soup that had gone cold.

The dinner passed in a blur. Luke ate heartily of the soup, thinking it was a shame that that was all there was. So he was pleasantly surprised when a plateful of greens arrived next. But the courses that came after that were foods he had no hope of identifying. Once, he suspected he was eating white lumps of rice under some type of gravy. But Luke was pretty certain that the gravy wasn't made from pork fat, which was the only kind he'd ever eaten before.

He supposed the food was good—delicious, even—but it was hard to enjoy it sitting with a sullen Smits and Smits's icy parents. And an army of servants constantly came in and out, whisking dishes away as soon as any of them were finished. By the ninth course Luke was aware of a strange sensation in his stomach: He was too full.

"Psst, Lee," Smits finally whispered from across the table. "You don't have to eat it *all.*"

Luke noticed that the others were barely touching their food, letting the servants take away plates missing only a bite or two.

"Oh," Luke said. He wondered what happened to the extra food. Did the servants eat it? Was it thrown away?

No one would be able to tell from the Grants' dining habits that there'd been famines and starvation barely fifteen years earlier, that food was still rationed across the land. Luke had a feeling that the Grants hadn't paid any attention to the famines at all.

Except for Smits's quick whisper, there was no chatter at the table, no questions from the parents, like, "How's school going?" or "When do you suppose they'll have the wiring fixed at Hendricks?" For all the notice Mr. and Mrs. Grant gave Smits and Luke, you'd almost have thought the boys were still away at school.

The Grants didn't even speak to the servants who brought and removed the food. For all the notice they gave to the servants, Luke wondered if they thought that the food appeared and disappeared by magic.

Finally, finally, the servants brought ice cream, which Luke was sure had to be the last course. In spite of his now aching stomach, he ate all of his ice cream, down to the last drop. Ice cream had been such a treat back home. He'd had it only once or twice in his life.

"Lee," Mrs. Grant hissed. "Gentlemen do not *gobble.*"

Red faced, Luke dropped his spoon. It clattered on the floor, spinning off threads of melted ice cream across the polished marble.

"May I be excused?" Smits asked in the silence that followed.

Mrs. Grant nodded.

Luke watched a servant swoop out of nowhere, grab up the spoon, and wipe away the ice cream in a flash. He gathered his nerve to speak.

"May I be excused, too?" he asked.

"I suppose," Mrs. Grant said.

Heavyhearted, Luke found his way back to Lee's room.

He threw himself across the bed, fighting waves of nausea. He'd hated Hendricks School at first, too, but the Grants' house seemed much, much worse. And yet Smits had seemed to be trying to help him. And Oscar had appeared at just the right moment to help him with that tie.

Why? Why did either of them care what happened to Luke?

CHAPTER *TWENTY*

Luke was sound asleep, and had been for hours, when someone began shaking his shoulder.

"Lee. Get up," a voice whispered.

Luke opened his eyes to complete darkness. It was the middle of the night, he thought. He'd fallen asleep without changing his clothes, so the knot of the bow tie dug uncomfortably into his neck. He'd been dreaming, he realized, about nooses.

"Wha—who are you?" he said, fighting a sense of total disorientation.

"Shh!" A hand clapped instantly over Luke's mouth. He'd accidentally spoken out loud. "Don't make another noise. So help me, I'll . . ." A tiny penlight switched on in the darkness. "I'm your . . . father. See?"

Mr. Grant held the tiny light below his chin, illuminating his face. But the effect was ghoulish, creating eerie shadows around his eyes. Luke felt like he was looking into a Halloween mask.

"Now, come with me," Mr. Grant whispered.

Timidly Luke slipped first one foot, then the other, out of bed. He had a flash of memory—this was like all those nights he'd been awakened by Oscar, summoned by Smits. And he'd always gone. What if he'd disobeyed? What if, just once, he'd stamped his foot and announced, "You know what? I'm not Lee, and I'm not going to pretend anymore. Leave me alone. Let me go back to sleep."

But he couldn't have done that any of the other times, and he couldn't do it now.

Silently, fighting a rising sense of dread, Luke walked alongside Mr. Grant. They went out of his room, down the hall, down the stairs. Luke might have suspected Mr. Grant of purposely leading him in circles, trying to confuse him. But the house was so much like a maze, even in bright daylight, that Luke figured Mr. Grant was truly taking the most direct route to wherever he was going.

Finally Mr. Grant stood before a closed door on the first level. Luke wasn't entirely sure, but he thought that he'd attempted to open this door earlier in the day, when he'd been exploring. The door had been locked then. But now Mr. Grant looked around cautiously, opened the door effortlessly, and motioned Luke inside. A few seconds later Mr. Grant stepped in behind him and shut the door.

"Have you activated the system?" a woman's voice asked in the darkness.

"Three, two, one . . . all set," Mr. Grant said.

Lights came on then. They were standing in an office. A massive mahogany desk stood in the center of the room, and bookshelves lined the walls. Mrs. Grant was sitting in a stiff chair in front of the desk, but she quickly stood up and walked toward Luke and Mr. Grant.

"Finally," she said.

Luke tensed, afraid that she was going to hug him again. But she only took him by the shoulders, held him at arm's length, and squinted thoughtfully at him.

"Braces, of course," she said. "And perhaps some hair dye . . ."

"Maybe contacts," Mr. Grant said.

"Do you think anyone would really notice his eyes? They're not that different," Mrs. Grant said. "Having him fitted for contacts, that'd be another person we'd have to pay off—"

"Of course. You're right," Mr. Grant said.

Luke felt like he was an object they were considering buying. Neither of them had looked him square in the eye yet or addressed him directly. Didn't they think he would have any say in the matters of braces, hair dye, or contacts?

No. Of course not.

Finally Mrs. Grant stepped back and said, "Well, *I* think

it will work. I think we ought to try it."

"Nothing to lose, eh?" Mr. Grant said.

Luke struggled to find his voice. "What do you want from me?" he demanded.

Mrs. Grant looked back at him, very solemnly, and announced, "We want you to die."

CHAPTER *TWENTY-ONE*

Luke jerked back and made a panicky grab for the door. But the doorknob had vanished somehow.

"Oh, very nice, Sarinia," Mr. Grant said. "Now you've terrified him. She doesn't mean for *real*," he told Luke. "We just want to stage your death so—well, it's a long story."

"Tell me," Luke said through gritted teeth.

Mr. Grant frowned at Mrs. Grant.

"This isn't the way to get started," he said. "You'll have to forgive us. We're still a little . . . grief stricken. It's been very hard for us today, dealing with another boy pretending to be Lee. . . ."

Luke looked around frantically. It was the middle of the night, and for once there were no servants in sight. Still, his heart began pounding with fear at the thought that someone might have heard Mr. Grant say that Luke wasn't Lee.

"It's all right," Mr. Grant said soothingly. "This is a soundproof, secure room. We can speak openly here."

"Have a seat," Mrs. Grant offered, turning a chair toward Luke. "We'll explain."

Luke was thinking that a soundproof, secure room would be a great place to kill someone. But what could he do? He sat down.

Mr. and Mrs. Grant sat down, too, in chairs opposite his. Mrs. Grant leaned forward.

"Our son Lee was a wonderful boy," she began in a sad voice. "Everything a parent could want. He was good at sports, musically gifted, a top student. . . ." She paused to dab at her eyes. "But he was a bit, um, idealistic."

"He was a troublemaker," Mr. Grant said harshly. "Stubborn as a rock. From the day he was born, he thought he could run the world."

Luke tried to make those two descriptions fit together. So Lee had been a perfect, gifted, stubborn troublemaker.

"Like father, like son. Right, dear?" Mrs. Grant purred.

"Aah . . ." Mr. Grant waved her question away. "When he died, he was, um, breaking the law ever so slightly," Mr. Grant continued. "He was—well, there's no need for you to know the whole story. But suffice it to say that it would have been a bit difficult for us to explain the circumstances of his death."

If Luke had only been a little braver, he might have asked, "Did the Government really kill him?" But Mrs. Grant had already taken over the conversation.

"And when he died, as you can imagine, we were distraught," Mrs. Grant added. "Simply overcome."

She sniffed daintily and let Mr. Grant continue the explanation.

"So when our friend George Talbot approached us with a possible solution, a way to make it look as though Lee *hadn't* died—and, by the way, to help you—we surely couldn't be faulted for taking advantage of that opportunity. Could we?" Mr. Grant asked.

He sounded as though he truly expected Luke to answer. Like he wanted to know what Luke thought.

"Um, no," Luke said. "And believe me, I was happy to . . ." It didn't seem right to say he was happy when they were talking about their son dying. "I mean, I'm very grateful that you made the decision you did."

"Right. And you've had, what—five, six months now of using Lee's name?" Mr. Grant asked.

"Five months, three weeks, and two days," Mrs. Grant said faintly.

Luke could only nod. Lee's mother knew exactly how long it had been since Lee died. Somehow that made Lee seem real, as much as if Luke had found pictures Lee had drawn, letters he had written, initials he had carved in his room.

Luke had liked it better before, when Lee Grant was only a name to him, a name he could hate if he wanted to.

"So here's the thing," Mr. Grant said, ignoring his wife. "We've given you these past several months of freedom. So we're just asking a small favor in return. Smits—our other son, Smits—has had quite a few problems accepting his brother's death. We asked him to keep the news secret, but—"

"Maybe it was too much to expect. Maybe it was too much to expect of anyone," Mrs. Grant said, almost to herself.

Luke could tell which one of them had decided to hide Lee's death.

"We hired a bodyguard for him," Mr. Grant continued. "We let him go meet you. We thought that might help somehow. But he's only getting worse."

Luke wondered how the Grants could know that. Had Oscar told them about Smits setting the fire? Had Smits confided in his parents?

Luke couldn't imagine Smits telling Mr. and Mrs. Grant anything personal at all.

"So we came up with an alternate plan," Mr. Grant said. "We thought we'd have some parties, show you off very publicly as Lee, and then—"

"Do I look like Lee?" Luke asked quietly.

He wanted Mr. Grant to pull a picture out of a billfold or off the top of his desk. Suddenly he desperately wanted to see what the real Lee had looked like. If only he could see the real Lee, he thought, he could decide for himself whether Lee had been a troublemaker, as his father said, or the brilliant saint Mrs. Grant had described. It mattered, suddenly.

Lee Grant, who were you?

"We think you could pass as Lee," Mrs. Grant said with

a catch in her voice. "We think. We've been debating this issue all day."

"Can I see—," Luke began, but Mr. Grant interrupted.

"Anyhow, as I was saying, we'd show you off, then stage your death. Then Smits—and Mrs. Grant and I—could grieve openly. And there'd be no danger of anyone accusing Lee of dying during any, um, illegal activities last April, because everyone would just have seen you now. In September."

Luke considered not being Lee anymore. It would actually be a relief to take on some other anonymous name—some name that didn't come with the complications of a grieving brother and powerful parents. Still, he remembered Mr. Hendricks's worries about Luke taking a name that might save some other third child in hiding, or of taking a name that carried even more danger than Lee Grant's. He wondered if he could still go back to Hendricks if he used a different name.

"Isn't there some other way to help Smits?" Luke asked. "If you kept him at home, and you talked about Lee, just the three of you—"

"What would the servants think?" Mrs. Grant asked.

"You could talk in here," Luke said hesitantly. "You could help him yourself, in private." He couldn't quite see the Grants, all cozy and grieving together. Crying together. He couldn't picture Mrs. Grant hugging Smits, or even Mrs. Grant hugging Mr. Grant. And he couldn't see this room as a place for comfort. It was too cold, too formal, too clearly a place for business deals and crafty thoughts, not raw emotions.

"No, no, you don't understand." Mr. Grant waved away Luke's suggestion. "You're just a child. You don't know what you're talking about. You'll just have to follow our plan."

"I suppose Mr. Talbot could find another fake identity for me," Luke said reluctantly.

"Oh, no," Mrs. Grant said. "You couldn't get another identity. Not after being seen as Lee. Someone might recognize you. And then where would we be?"

Luke stared at her in horror. "Then, what would happen to me? Where could I go without Lee's I.D. card?"

Mrs. Grant shrugged. "Well, wherever you were before you began passing yourself off as Lee." She made it sound like Luke had stolen Lee's identity—like he'd maybe even killed Lee himself.

"You want me to go back into hiding?" Lee asked incredulously.

And Mrs. Grant looked straight back at him and said, "Of course."

CHAPTER TWENTY-TWO

For just an instant Luke let himself imagine hiding again. He could go back home with Mother and Dad, Matthew and Mark. But he'd be living in the attic, taking his meals on the stairs again, out of sight. He wouldn't be allowed to look out windows or even to walk past a window.

"I can't," Luke said weakly. "I can't go back into hiding."

"Why not?" Mr. Grant said. "You were hiding before you got Lee's name. What's the big deal about hiding now?"

"It's . . ." Luke could only shake his head. They were rich and powerful. How could they possibly understand? Having tasted freedom, having been brave, having volunteered to do something grand for the cause—he absolutely could not return now to the nothingness of life in hiding. "How would you like it if someone told you that you had to go into hiding?" he asked the Grants.

Mrs. Grant stood up with a flounce.

"Oh, this is ridiculous," she said. "I've never had to hide. I'm a legal individual. I have rights. I'm a *Baron*. It's not the same."

"Don't you think I should have rights, too?" Luke asked.

Then, looking at the two adults' stony faces, he began to lose hope. They didn't care about third children. They'd never thought about whether Luke or anyone else like him should have rights or not. He was just a pawn to them, someone they could use for their own purposes and cast aside when they didn't need him anymore.

"That's not the point," Mrs. Grant said. "The point is . . ." A sly smile crept over her face. "The point is, it doesn't matter whether you like our plan or not. If you sabotage our plan, if you don't act like Lee, you sabotage yourself. Don't think we wouldn't be happy to call the Population Police on you."

She was threatening him. Luke felt the color drain from his cheeks. He stared into Mrs. Grant's exquisitely beautiful face, still perfectly made up at three in the morning. She was even still wearing a pearl necklace. What could he possibly say in response?

"But if you want me to help in staging my death . . . ," Luke began. He was ashamed that his voice came out in a whimper.

"Oh, don't you worry about that. We've got everything

planned. We don't need your cooperation," Mrs. Grant said with a sickly sweet smile.

And then the secret meeting was over, and Mr. Grant walked Luke back to his room—to Lee's room. In a daze Luke changed out of the rumpled tuxedo and into his own pajamas. And then he lay in bed, replaying the whole conversation in his mind. The more he thought about it, the more it seemed like a nightmare.

We want you to die. . . .

You couldn't get another identity. . . .

You were hiding before. . . . What's the big deal about hiding now?

The Grants might as well kill him for real and be done with it, Luke thought. Hiding again would be practically as bad as dying.

And then a resolve began to steal over him. No matter what, he wouldn't go back into hiding. Surely he could do something, secretly, as part of the underground resistance to the Government. Mr. Talbot had hinted before at the existence of secret workers for the cause. Luke wasn't sure if any of them had legal identities or not. He remembered three kids he'd met through his friend Nina—Percy, Matthias, and Alia. They'd once been involved in making fake I.D.'s. He wasn't sure what they were doing now, but maybe he could help them.

Luke's plans were vague and shadowy at best, but they made him feel better. He wasn't a Baron like the Grants, he wasn't legal like the Grants, he wasn't even an adult. But that didn't mean he had to roll over and play dead when they said to. That didn't mean he didn't have any choices. All he had to do was get in touch with Mr. Talbot, secretly. Mr. Talbot could protect him from the Grants' schemes.

CHAPTER *TWENTY-THREE*

Comforted by his plans, Luke had fallen back to sleep when someone began shaking his shoulders once again.

"Wake up!" a gruff voice whispered.

It was Oscar this time. Luke actually had the nerve to say, "We're home now. How can Smits be homesick?"

"Shh," Oscar said. "Follow me."

Mystified, Luke obeyed. But Oscar didn't lead Luke next door to Smits's room. He guided Luke on a convoluted path through the entire house. Only when they stood before a dark door did Luke realize: Oscar had led him back to the secret office.

"Wh—," Luke began.

"Shh!" Oscar said again, urgently.

He didn't look around the way Mr. Grant had, only jammed a key in the lock. The door swung open and Oscar yanked Luke inside. Oscar seemed to be pressing buttons the same way Mr. Grant had. The lights came on once again and, Luke noticed this time, the doorknob vanished. Somehow the door seemed to have turned into a smooth wall.

"How—how did you know about this room?" Luke asked.

"Lee told me," Oscar said. "Lee gave me a key."

Lee. Luke gulped.

"I'm Lee," he said without much conviction. "I never said a word to you about, um, our house. I've never given you anything."

Oscar gave Luke a look that almost seemed compassionate.

"We're in a soundproof room," he said. "We both know the truth. There's no need for lies here."

Stunned, Luke sank into a chair, the same one he'd sat in with the Grants.

"Don't worry," Oscar said. "I'm on your side. We're fighting for the same cause."

"How do I know that?" Luke asked. "Why should I trust you?"

To his surprise, Oscar laughed. "Tough little brat, aren't you? Not like that namby-pamby rich boy I'm supposed to be guarding all the time. You're not really a Baron, are you? Let me guess." Oscar narrowed his eyes, staring directly at Luke. "You grew up poor, I bet. Really, really poor. Like me. I just don't know how *you* were picked to take over Lee Grant's identity."

Luke didn't tell him. He stared straight back at Oscar.

Defiantly. But he felt as though Oscar had seen past the fancy silk Baron pajamas, monogrammed with Lee Grant's initials. Somehow Oscar knew that Luke was nobody—and not really brave, not really confident, not really rich.

Oscar shrugged, as if he hadn't really expected Luke to tell him anything. Or as if he didn't need to know more about Luke.

"I'm going to tell you a story," Oscar said softly. "Then you'll know why you should trust me. I'm sure you'll appreciate hearing the truth."

Oscar sat down opposite Luke. Oscar was wearing sweatpants and a T-shirt that emphasized his bulging biceps, but somehow he didn't seem like a muscle-bound bodyguard anymore. He looked downright thoughtful, squinting seriously at Luke.

"The Government wants people to think that everyone's in favor of our current dictator—I mean, *president,*" Oscar said sardonically. "That everyone believes that everything he does is just so wonderful and so *right.* That everyone believes the Barons deserve the privileges they get and the rest of the people deserve squat. But you and me, we know differently, don't we?" When Luke didn't answer, Oscar repeated, "Don't we, *Lee*?"

"Yes," Luke whispered. He was still stunned by Oscar's transformation. Oscar wasn't the proper, rule-obsessed servant anymore. Even his voice sounded rougher.

"When something's unfair," Oscar said, "anyone with any gumption is going to fight it. Right?"

Luke nodded. He wanted to say, "Look, I struck a blow against the Government myself. I turned in an informer for the Population Police." He wanted to impress this new Oscar, suddenly.

But he wasn't sure Oscar would be impressed by anything Luke had done.

"I was eight when I put my first pipe bomb in a Baron's mailbox," Oscar said. "By the time I was twelve, I was stealing Barons' cars. Not for my own benefit—no way! My buddies and me, we'd push those cars into the river. Can you imagine the kind of splash a limo makes? And how the police flock to the shore? We were risking our lives for the cause."

Luke swallowed hard.

"So then Barons moved farther and farther out from the big cities," Oscar said. "They all got security fences, security guards. They went crying to the Government, 'Boo-hoo-hoo. Those vandals are out of control.' And the Government listened to them. They passed new laws—did you know that it's a bigger crime to destroy a Baron's property than to kill an ordinary person? It's true." Oscar lowered his voice, as if confiding a great secret in Luke. "And meanwhile, ordinary people are starving in the streets. . . ."

"That's not fair," Luke said in a small voice.

Oscar stood up and started to pace. "That's right, it's

not fair. That's why we're doing something about it."

"We are?" Luke asked. He wondered if Oscar was going to say anything about the unfair Population Law, which forced third children into hiding. That was something else the Government had done wrong. Did Oscar know about those kids, who had even more reason than Oscar to hate the Government? Did Oscar care?

Oscar paused in his pacing and gave Luke a glance that made Luke feel about as big as an insect. And as easily squashed.

"I've been working for the underground resistance for years," Oscar said. "Our sole goal is to overthrow the Government and the Barons, and to reestablish justice. Equity for all, that's our motto." Oscar rested his hands on the back of the chair he'd been sitting in. Luke could tell that Oscar only needed to flex a muscle or two and he could have torn the chair to shreds. But Oscar wasn't moving. He was watching Luke.

"You and I both know," Oscar said, "it's treason even to say that I oppose the Government. If you reported me, I'd deny everything. And there'd be no evidence to link me to any plots."

Luke could tell Oscar was waiting for Luke now, waiting for some sort of cue to go on.

"I won't report you," Luke said. "Why would I do that?"

"Good," Oscar said. "We understand each other."

He sat down again and seemed to relax back into his story.

"I'll admit," he said. "I was nothing but a two-bit punk

in the beginning. I was poor, uneducated—how could I be anything else? But then my friends and me, we got hooked up with some other rebels. Eggheads, we called them. They thought about stuff like political philosophy. Who needs it? But they had the money to do real damage. They taught us about having more of an impact than blowing up a few mailboxes, ruining a few cars, when the Barons could always buy new. They taught us about being subtle. They even trained some of us as accountants, computer experts, electricians, all the trades. So we could create even more problems for the Government and the Barons."

"Oh," Luke said.

"You know those electrical outages they kept having on the coast? We did that," Oscar said. "Entire cities, blacked out. Because of us."

Luke had never heard of the electrical outages, but he tried to look impressed.

Oscar sprawled in his chair, as if he was totally comfortable with telling Luke this part of his story.

"Nobody was supposed to know about us, but we were famous, in our own way," Oscar said. "Who else dared to do anything? We were cool. We even started attracting a Baron kid or two, rebelling against their parents."

Luke looked up, startled.

"Lee," Luke said.

"Yep," Oscar said, nodding. "The real Lee Grant. Or

maybe I should say, the original version."

Luke leaned forward, waiting. He realized he was barely breathing.

"Lee wasn't our first Baron kid, but he had the best connections," Oscar said.

"But why would he—," Luke began.

"If your dad's the richest man in the country, and you're mad at him, what's the best way to get back at him? Mess up the Government. Such fun." Oscar shook his head. "None of us trusted him."

"Then, why did you let him join?" Luke asked.

"Don't you see?" Oscar asked. "He was Lee *Grant*. What a great weapon for our cause." He looked down. "Some in our group thought the best thing we could do was to kidnap him and ask for ransom. We could have financed our operations for years to come."

"But you didn't do that," Luke said, almost as a question.

"No," Oscar said impatiently. "We thought he'd be more useful in other ways. And he was. He . . . matured. He was turning into a fine subversive. When he was home on break from school, he relayed lots of plans he stole from his father. Plans that helped us know what the Government was up to so we could counter their activities."

"What did he do for you when he was away at school?" Luke asked. In spite of himself, he was fascinated by this new version of Lee's life. Luke felt like he was putting together a jigsaw puzzle: Here's one piece showing Lee pulling his younger brother, Smits, in a red wagon. Here's the piece from his mother: Lee as the gifted musician, the talented athlete, the brilliant student. Here's the piece from Mr. Grant—Lee as the stubborn troublemaker.

Somehow that was the only piece that seemed to jibe with Oscar's story.

"He went to one of those fancy, richy-rich prep schools. And while he was there"—Oscar chucked—"he tricked all those sons of the establishment into helping us without even knowing it. He was a piece of work, that Lee."

"But he died," Luke said. For the first time he put together what Smits and Smits's parents had said. "He was killed doing something for you. For your group." It wasn't a question. That had to be the "illegal activity" Mr. Grant had referred to. That had to be the reason a Government soldier had shot Lee. Smits hadn't been lying about that at all.

Oscar frowned.

"Unfortunately, yes. He was killed during one of our secret missions," Oscar said.

"What was it?"

Oscar narrowed his eyes, as if trying to decide how much to tell Luke. "Last spring we thought maybe we had our chance to act. There'd been an anti-Government rally in the capital. We weren't part of that—we knew it was doomed from the start. But it shook some people up. A lot of kids died, right there in public, and there were actually some officials who got upset. Public deaths are so much more offensive than private ones."

Luke wasn't sure what to make of this news. Was Oscar talking about the rally that Jen had led and died in? Had the rally had an impact after all?

"We thought we'd strike while the enemy was in disarray," Oscar said. "But we had to get weapons out to everyone in our group as quickly as possible. Some of our people were in the far north. Lee was a good cross-country skier. He volunteered to cross the mountains to deliver the munitions."

"Munitions?" Luke repeated.

"Guns," Oscar said.

Luke tried to imagine a boy his age, alone in the mountains, carrying guns. He'd never seen any mountains for real, but he pictured them as desolate places. Just snow and trees and Lee, carrying guns.

"So they caught him. The Government caught him," Luke said.

Oscar nodded. "Lee had the sense to try to escape. He knew this was life or death. If they'd captured him alive, they might have tortured him. He might have revealed our plans, betrayed our group. We might all be dead right now if Lee had talked."

If Luke had been in Lee's place, would Luke have been able to be so brave?

"But your plan," Luke said. "You didn't go through with your plan?"

"Do you see any sign that the Government's gone? That

the Barons' wealth has been given to the people?" Oscar clutched the arm of his chair—an exquisite leather chair—as if he really wanted to hand it to some poor person. "No. Without our allies in the north, with the Government suspicious after finding Lee, it wasn't worth the risk."

"Oh," Luke said.

All this had been happening while Luke was sitting at home wondering what had happened at Jen's rally. What else had been going on in the country then? How many others wanted to overthrow the Government? Maybe if they all got together—maybe that way something would happen.

"Did Mr. Talbot know about your plan?" Luke asked.

"Who?" Oscar said.

"Mr. Talbot. The man who came to school that one time. He had lunch with Mr. Hendricks and Smits and me, the day Smits ran off and said he wouldn't obey his parents. . . ."

A disgusted look was spreading over Oscar's face.

"He's a Baron. Barons can't be trusted," Oscar said.

"You trusted Lee," Luke reminded him.

"Lee was a kid," Oscar said. "He could be . . . molded. Someone like this Mr. Talbot—bah!"

Luke felt honor-bound to defend Jen's father.

"But he's helped me," Luke protested. "More than once." Did he dare tell Oscar that Mr. Talbot was a double agent, pretending to work for the Population Police while he secretly sabotaged their work?

"Are you sure?" Oscar snarled. "Are you sure he wasn't just helping himself? Will he still help you when you no longer serve his purposes?"

And Luke couldn't answer that. He trusted Mr. Talbot. Of course he trusted Mr. Talbot. But maybe it had helped Mr. Talbot to give Luke a fake I.D., to protect him at Hendricks School. Luke knew about Jen. Luke could tell the Population Police about Jen. Luke could get Mr. Talbot killed.

It had never occurred to Luke before that he had any power over Mr. Talbot.

He didn't like thinking about Mr. Talbot in that way. He forced himself to stare back steadily at Oscar, so Oscar didn't see how confused Luke was. Luke crossed his arms over his chest, trying to look certain, trying to look unfazed. Something in his pajama pocket jabbed into his arm—it was the fake I.D.'s he'd taken from Smits's room at Hendricks after the fire. Did Luke dare ask Oscar about those I.D.'s now? Was it finally time to get an explanation?

No. Luke felt like he'd already made a mistake mentioning Mr. Talbot. It was better to wait and see what Oscar would tell him on his own.

After a second Oscar sighed and said, "Never mind. This Mr. Talbot, he doesn't matter now. It helped everyone to have you become Lee Grant. It helped the Grants and it helped our cause. It protected us from the Government."

Luke could have added, "And it helped me." He could even have made it funny, like a joke. That would have defused the tension that had suddenly arisen between him and Oscar. But he couldn't bring himself to do that. He kept his lips resolutely pressed together, waiting.

"Yes, you helped us all," Oscar said. "But there have been problems. . . ."

"I know about Smits," Luke said. That seemed to be a safe subject. "I know that he told people Lee was dead—"

Oscar waved away that concern. "We can handle Smits. He's just a little boy. And he has me to watch out for him." Oscar grinned in a way that reminded Luke of a drawing of the Big Bad Wolf in the fairy tale book his mother had read to him when he was little. Hadn't there been a story in that book about how stupid it was to let a wolf guard sheep?

"Do Mr. and Mrs. Grant know that you, um, I mean . . . ," Luke began.

"That I know how Lee died? That I know Smits isn't so crazy after all—just stupid? That I work for the resistance? Do you think *I'm* crazy?" Oscar peered intently at Luke, and for a minute Luke thought he expected an answer. Then Oscar exploded, "Of course not. They don't know anything."

"Well, that's good," Luke muttered.

Oscar laughed. "Yeah, you could say that. I just 'happened' to show up here looking for work at the right time. 'Do you need a bodyguard for your sons?' I asked. 'Sons,' I said, even though I knew Lee was already dead. And it just so happened I had perfect credentials. . . ." He smirked. "Perfect *fake* credentials, of course."

"Oh," Luke said. He frowned. "Then if the Grants don't know, and you're not worried about Smits—what's the problem?"

"The Grants are being blackmailed," Oscar said.

Luke looked back blankly at Oscar. "Blackmailed? Is that where—"

Oscar didn't wait for Luke to figure out the meaning. "Someone knows what really happened to Lee. And he—or they, whoever it is—has been threatening to reveal the truth to the Government if the Grants don't pay lots of money."

Luke stared at Oscar. This wasn't just about the Grants and Lee. This was his life on the line, too.

"Are they paying it?" Luke asked.

"So far," Oscar said. "But they want to stop."

And suddenly Luke understood. Suddenly he knew why he'd been taken away from Hendricks School, why the Grants had called him into the secret room only a few hours ago, why they suddenly had a use for him after months of ignoring him.

"That's why they want me to pretend to die," Luke said. "They don't care about Smits or grieving at all. They're just trying to stop the blackmail. It's all about money." He was perfectly willing to believe the worst about the Grants. But then he remembered—should he have revealed so much to Oscar?

But Oscar was nodding grimly. He clearly knew all about the Grants' plan.

"I suspected that that was what they were telling you tonight," Oscar said. "Well, don't worry. You're not going to die. Smits is going to die in your place."

CHAPTER TWENTY-FOUR

For the longest time Luke could only stare wordlessly at Oscar. Then he managed to croak, "Just pretend, right?"

"Oh, right," Oscar said quickly. "We're going to fake Smits's death, the way the Grants were planning to fake yours. After that, the Grants wouldn't dare let anything happen to you, because it would look too suspicious to have two sons die in bizarre accidents. And as Lee Grant, you can help the cause. Think of all you can do from this base of operations. They couldn't stop you. . . ."

Luke remembered what Mr. Hendricks had said before Smits came to Luke's school: "I'd have a better chance of stopping the wind than stopping a Grant from doing what he wants." What if Luke could really act like Lee Grant, could really carry off that kind of overwhelming power? He could almost believe in Oscar's fantasy. Almost.

"But what would happen to Smits?" Luke asked.

"Oh, we'd hide him away somewhere," Oscar said. "Not

that it matters. He's such a worthless brat."

Luke tried to imagine Smits in hiding. He'd been miserable enough at Hendricks, which was a paradise of freedom compared with life in hiding. How could Luke force Smits into the same prison Luke had escaped?

"Isn't there some other choice?" Luke asked hesitantly. "Can't you just stop the Grants' plan without hurting Smits?"

Oscar laughed. "Do you really care whether Smits gets hurt or not? This is *war*. Nothing's going to be accomplished without someone getting hurt. Why shouldn't it be Smits? Is there someone else you'd prefer to see in pain?"

Luke went cold. Was Oscar threatening him? Did Oscar care who got hurt? Would he care if somebody died?

"I don't want anyone hurt," Luke said in a small voice. "Can't we do this . . . peacefully?"

This time Oscar's laughter was overwhelming. It took him a full five minutes to regain control.

"Oh, puh-lease," Oscar said, still snorting laughter. "Do you avoid stepping on ants, too? Maybe I misjudged you. I didn't take you for a sissy. I didn't take you for a Baron lover. Just another drone supporting the ruling class and the Government—"

"I don't support the Government," Luke said angrily.

"Well, sure, you can *say* that," Oscar taunted him. "But I'm giving you a chance to strike a blow for freedom, and you're scared some spoiled Baron brat might get treated a little roughly. What's Smits to you, anyway? What's he ever done for you?"

"Nothing," Luke said, but it wasn't true. Luke couldn't forget the slow unreeling of confidences Smits had told Luke all those nights back at school. Smits had shared all his memories of the real Lee. Luke had never asked for them. They didn't make Smits any less infuriating. But Luke couldn't forget them. He couldn't forget that Smits wasn't just a Baron, but a real boy, already deeply hurt, already deep in grief.

How could Luke be responsible for hurting him more?

"We don't have to decide anything tonight, do we?" Luke asked. "Mr. and Mrs. Grant said they were going to dye my hair and get me braces. Nothing's going to happen right away. We have time to think this out. Maybe—maybe if we work together we can think of a better plan. . . ."

Oscar snorted.

"I thought someone like you would jump at the chance to help the cause. I thought you were like me," he said. "I thought you had guts."

"I do!" Luke wanted to say. "I am! I would!" But the words wouldn't come. Because he wasn't sure. Of anything.

Oscar didn't give him a chance to interrupt.

"Don't you see?" Oscar said. "You don't always get time to think, time to consider carefully. We have an opportunity now that we can take or we can miss. And if we miss it, what happens then?" He stared straight at Luke. "I need your answer tonight. Are you with me or not?"

Luke gulped.

"I don't know," he said. That seemed to be the bravest answer he could give. It was, at least, honest.

But what place did honesty have around people like Oscar and the Grants?

It was too hard to sit there with Oscar staring at him, waiting for him to decide. Abruptly Luke stood up.

"What are you doing?" Oscar said.

"Um, going back to bed?" No matter how hard Luke tried to sound strong and certain—as tough as Oscar—his voice rose into a question. "I'm—I mean, a good night's sleep will help me think. Could you open the door for me, please?"

Luke was practically begging. Oscar had all the power now. If he wanted to, Oscar could keep Luke prisoner until Luke agreed to help him. What would Luke do then?

But Oscar stood up, too.

"Just one word of advice before you go," Oscar said. "Watch out for chandeliers."

CHAPTER *TWENTY-FIVE*

Luke woke to bright sunlight streaming in the windows. This, too, seemed fake somehow—like a trick. How could the sun be shining when Luke's mind was in such turmoil? He looked up at the elaborate light fixture that arced over his bed, and even that seemed dangerous this morning. "Watch out for chandeliers," Oscar had said. Did the light over his bed count as a chandelier? Was Luke in danger every time he went to sleep?

Luke shook his head back and forth on the pillow. He needed to get a grip on his fears. He remembered what Mother always said back home every time he or his brothers whined about anything: "Count your blessings. Look on the bright side." Luke's current problems were a lot worse than, say, Matthew and Mark wanting to play football while Luke wanted to play tag. But maybe he could find a few blessings even now. He began making a mental list.

1. Oscar had been kind enough to warn Luke about the chandelier.

But why? Was it a true warning or just a trick?

Luke decided to move on to the next blessing.

2. Nobody was going to blow his cover. The Grants needed him to be Lee. Oscar needed him to be Lee.

But what about Smits? Could Luke trust Smits to keep Luke's secret?

Luke frowned and abandoned his list of blessings. It was all too confusing. Every blessing hid more danger and uncertainty. It was like the reverse of that saying about clouds and silver linings: All of Luke's silver linings hid dark storm clouds.

I'll just call Mr. Talbot, Luke told himself. *He'll know what to do.*

"He's a Baron. Barons can't be trusted. . . ." Oscar's words from the night before echoed in Luke's head. Luke tried to push them away, but the doubts lingered.

Luke wished he could trust Oscar. Oscar was already right there. He didn't like the Grants any more than Luke did. It would be so easy to agree with Oscar, let Oscar do all the planning, let Oscar save Luke.

If only Oscar's plan didn't involve Smits. How could Luke, who wanted freedom so badly, help send another boy into hiding?

And was that what Oscar was really planning to do?

In that moment before Luke had asked about Oscar's plan, "Just pretend, right?" he'd seen a glimmer in Oscar's eyes.

If Luke hadn't protested, would Oscar have let him believe that Smits was going to be killed for real?

Was Oscar planning actual murder?

Were the Grants?

Luke had been wrong about a good night's sleep helping him think. His thoughts were more jumbled than ever. He was more terrified than ever.

"I *can* trust Mr. Talbot," he said aloud fiercely.

He slipped out of bed and went into the hall. He tapped on Smits's door.

"Who is it?" Smits mumbled.

"Me," Luke said. It was too hard to say Lee's name to Smits. Especially now. Without waiting for an answer, Luke pushed on in.

"Ever heard of privacy?" Smits said. "Ever heard of letting someone sleep in?"

Smits was still in bed, tangled up in his blankets and sheets as if he'd been fighting with his bedding all night long. His hair stuck up at odd angles, making him seem younger than ever. He was just a little kid. After having heard Oscar's plan, Luke found it hurt just to look at Smits.

But Luke took a deep breath and reminded himself that he was supposed to be a carefree Baron, lazing around on an unexpected day off from school. Not an illegal third child terrified of murder plots.

"It's ten o'clock already," Luke said. "How much sleep do you need?"

He was proud of the way his voice sounded so even and calm—even playful.

Smits just groaned.

"Hey," Luke said, still forcing himself to sound casual. "Don't you think we should call back to school and see how close they are to finishing the repairs? See how soon we can go—I mean, we'll have to go back?"

Luke had picked this ruse on the spur of the moment. It'd be easier to get Mr. Hendricks to seek help from Mr. Talbot, rather than trying to call Mr. Talbot directly. Nobody could deny a boy a phone if he said he just wanted to call his school. Could they?

Smits stared back at Luke as if Smits had totally forgotten about Hendricks School. Then he laughed.

"Oh, good try," he said. "But Dad'll see through it."

"What?" Luke said, suddenly scared that even Smits had figured out what Luke was planning.

"You want to make some more of those prank calls again, don't you?" Smits asked. "Remember how much trouble we got into last year at Christmas? 'Hello, is your refrigerator running? Can't you catch it?' And then Dad made it so we couldn't use any of the phones in the house at all, because they all take a special code?"

Smits was covering for Luke once again, telling him

information that Lee would have known, but Luke didn't. Why? Why did Smits want to help Luke?

It didn't matter. Either way, Luke wouldn't be able to use a phone.

"We're basically prisoners here, aren't we?" Luke asked quietly.

At that moment Oscar stepped into the room. Luke froze.

"Ah," Oscar said. "A little early-morning brotherly chitchat, I see. How pleasant." He leaned casually against the wall. Then he very deliberately pulled a headset off his ears and placed it on a chest of drawers beside him. "I won't need this now that I'm right in the room with the two of you."

Luke glanced at Smits, wondering if the younger boy got the message, too: Oscar had been listening to their entire conversation. Smits's room was bugged, and Oscar heard everything that happened there electronically.

Smits's face registered no surprise whatsoever.

"Yeah, it was pleasant until you showed up," Smits said.

Luke looked from Smits to Oscar. He felt trapped between the two of them, the muscular man and the scrawny boy. Oscar wanted Luke to betray Smits. And Smits wanted—what?

"Sometimes brothers have secrets they want to share," Oscar said. "And sometimes they have secrets they need to keep to themselves."

And Luke saw, staring at Smits's face, that Smits

thought Oscar was saying that for Smits's sake, telling Smits not to share any secrets with Luke.

What secrets did Smits know?

And what had Oscar told him?

CHAPTER TWENTY-SIX

Luke took a shower and got dressed. For some reason he couldn't have explained, even to himself, he transferred the fake I.D.'s for Oscar and Smits from his pajamas into the pants he'd put on. Maybe he just liked having a few secrets of his own. Or—how did he know that his room wasn't going to be searched while he was away?

Being at the Grants' house was making him totally paranoid.

Except—was it still paranoia if all his fears were justified?

On the way down to breakfast Luke passed Oscar on the stairs. Luke half expected him to stop Luke and ask quietly, "So what's your answer now?"

But Oscar only flickered his gaze briefly in Luke's direction. Otherwise, he acted as if Luke didn't exist.

He took my "I don't know" as a no, Luke thought. *And the chance to join his cause was a onetime offer.* Luke's heart sank. He wanted to grab the hulking man and beg for a second chance. But how could he? He still didn't want to hurt Smits.

"What's going to happen now?" Luke asked weakly. He meant, "Are you going to kill Smits or just hide him away somewhere? Or are the Grants going to kill me?"

Oscar didn't answer, just brushed on by.

Luke stood still, practically trembling. *Breakfast,* he told himself. *I'll feel better after breakfast.* He forced himself to continue down the stairs.

But after a huge meal that he barely tasted, he could think of nothing to do except wander aimlessly around the house. In the living room—actually, one of several rooms that Luke would have called a living room—he found an elegantly curved telephone sitting on a coffee table. Without hope, he picked up the receiver.

A maid appeared out of nowhere and scolded, "Now, Master Lee, you know your father's got those secret codes on that."

Luke got an idea.

"Tell me the code," he said. "You're the servant. I'm Master Lee. You have to tell me the code."

The maid laughed. "Sure, and you think I'd know it?" She shook a feather duster playfully at him. "Now, scoot. I've got dusting to do."

Embarrassed, Luke turned away. Master Lee. Right. And Oscar thought that if Smits was out of the way, Luke could manipulate the Grants into serving the cause?

No, Luke realized. Oscar thought he could manipulate Luke into manipulating the Grants. Luke's only choices were between being a pawn for the Grants and being a pawn for Oscar.

But Luke couldn't even choose between those two options, because he didn't know how or when the Grants or Oscar intended to carry out their plans. Why hadn't he pretended to be more cooperative during both of his sessions in the secret room? Why hadn't he just lied like everyone else?

Luke sank down onto the nearest couch. He couldn't call Mr. Talbot or Mr. Hendricks. He couldn't trust anyone at the Grants' house. He couldn't stop any of the plots boiling around him. He couldn't even tell the difference between the lies and the truths that he'd heard. For all he knew, Oscar might be working for the Government, not the resistance. Smits might always have hated his older brother, Lee. The Grants might be the poorest people in the country, instead of the richest. Or, no—Luke stared down at the finely woven carpet beneath his feet—the Grants' wealth was one fact that was indisputable.

"Lee! There you are!" Mrs. Grant suddenly swooped into the room. Lee instantly sat up straight, but she frowned anyway. "For heaven's sake, get off that couch this instant. You'll leave it rumpled, and how would that look for our party this evening?"

Luke bolted to his feet.

"P-p-party?" he asked.

"Oh, yes," Mrs. Grant said. "It'll be the social event of the season. We've been planning it for months. It's so nice that you and Smits are home from school and will be able to attend. Isn't it?"

She smiled so sweetly at him that Luke had a hard time remembering how coldly she'd regarded him the night before.

"Is it—do we . . ." Luke wanted to ask if Smits and Lee had usually attended their parents' big parties before. He wanted to ask if he'd be expected to know any of the other guests, and if so, what he was supposed to do when he met them tonight. But of course those weren't questions he could just blurt out, unless he was in the secret room. He settled for, "Do I have to wear a tux?"

Mrs. Grant laughed, making a sound that reminded Luke of breaking glass.

"Of course, you silly goose. You boys! Thinking you can get away without wearing a tux! Would you believe Smits asked me the same thing?"

And Luke looked back into Mrs. Grant's falsely sparkling eyes and thought, *No. I'm not sure I can believe you even when you tell me something as simple as that.*

"Now, come on," Mrs. Grant said. "The orthodontist and hairdresser are here. It's time for your makeover!"

CHAPTER *TWENTY-SEVEN*

By eight o'clock there were tiny lights strung in the trees along the driveway. An army of maids had made sure that every inch of the Grants' house was dust free and virtually gleaming. Dozens of cooks had prepared tray after tray of more foods than Luke had ever seen before.

And Luke had been transformed as well. Most of his teeth had been encased in silver prisons, with something that felt like barbed wire running between them. His hair had been dyed a darker brown, while Mrs. Grant had fluttered over the hairdresser, lamenting, "I can't believe you can't trust a *boy* anymore not to go bleaching his hair while he's away at school. . . ."

The braces hurt. His newly dyed—and gelled—hair felt stiff and unfamiliar. He didn't recognize himself when he walked past a mirror.

And now he and Smits were in their tuxes, standing at the top of the stairs. Waiting.

"I want both of you to make a grand entrance," Mrs.

Grant said, hovering over them, straightening Luke's tie, flattening a tiny cowlick at the back of Smits's head. "After all the guests have arrived, I'll have the butler announce you. He'll say, 'And here are the sons of the manor, Lee and Smithfield Grant.' And then you'll come down the stairs, like so."

She took small, mincing steps down the top few stairs before turning around to make sure that they had been listening. Was this part of the plot? Luke wondered. Were the Grants counting on his being so clumsy and unaccustomed to the spotlight that he'd trip and fall? Would the guests believe that he would die from such a fall?

Luke stared down the long stairway. Of course they would believe such a thing. If he tripped at the top and fell down thirty-two stairs, he might die for real.

And that would probably suit the Grants just fine.

Luke held in a shiver of fear and reminded himself: Chandeliers. Oscar had said that he needed to watch out for chandeliers. And assuming that Oscar was telling the truth about that, Luke had enough to worry about without looking for other death traps.

Far below, the front doorbell rang.

"That must be the first guests," Mrs. Grant said. "It'll be the Snodgrasses—they're always early. They have no social graces." Mrs. Grant shook her head disapprovingly and began walking down the stairs. She turned around briefly to remind both boys, "Now, remember. Be on your best behavior."

Down below, the butler was opening the door. Luke could hear his booming voice call out, "Ah, Mr. and Mrs. Snodgrass. Mr. and Mrs. Grant will be so glad to greet you. May I take your coats?"

Beside Luke, Smits slumped and sat down on the top step. Luke decided he might as well do the same. He slid down beside the younger boy. The fake I.D.'s he'd transferred into his tuxedo pocket poked his leg, as if he needed another reminder that everything around him was false.

"I can't believe they're having a party," Smits muttered. "My brother's dead, and they're having a party."

Luke glanced anxiously around. Oscar was leaning on a railing right behind them, but he seemed not to hear.

"It's been nearly six months," Luke said apologetically. "Probably that's long enough to wait before people start having parties again."

"They were having parties all along," Smits said glumly.

"They had to pretend . . . ," Luke started to say. He didn't like defending Mr. and Mrs. Grant, but he was getting panicked. Smits needed to pretend, too. What if Smits told one of the party guests that Lee was dead? What if one of the servants overheard?

"But they were enjoying themselves," Smits said fiercely. "They love their parties. They never cared about Lee."

In spite of himself Luke argued, "I thought you said they liked him better than you."

Smits fixed Luke with a dead stare. "So now you know what they think of me."

Behind them Oscar cleared his throat warningly. Luke was suddenly fed up with all the subterfuge. Without thinking, he turned around and asked Oscar, "Does Smits know who you are? Does Smits know that you knew Lee? That you can tell him everything he wants to know about how Lee died?"

Oscar's face turned a fiery red. He jerked his fists up; Luke knew that if even one of those fists hit him, he'd be knocked down the stairs for sure. But Oscar stopped just short of swinging at Luke.

Because Smits was answering.

With his eyes trained forward, Smits began reciting, "Oscar is my bodyguard. My parents hired him when I started telling lies at my old school. I'm not mentally stable. That's what my parents say. That's why I have Oscar. Oscar works for my parents."

He sounded like a schoolboy repeating facts he'd memorized but didn't understand. It was eerie.

"Good," Oscar growled. "Now we all know where we stand."

After that the three of them sat in silence at the top of the stairs until a huge light suddenly shone up at them, and the butler's booming voice called out, "And here are the sons of the mansion, Lee and Smithfield Grant."

Luke stumbled to his feet. Blindly he began descending the stairs beside Smits. The light was so intense, he couldn't see any of the guests below. But they were clapping. Luke tried to force himself to smile in the direction of the applause. The smile only pressed his lips more tightly into the braces, making his mouth ache even more.

At the bottom of the stairs Mrs. Grant wrapped first Luke, then Smits, into showy hugs. Smits wasn't slighted in the least this time.

"My sons," Mrs. Grant said, and she sounded as if she loved them both deeply.

An old, bewhiskered man behind her stepped forward to shake Luke's hand.

"My, how you've grown," the man said. "I haven't seen you since you were barely up to my knee."

"Yes, Mr. President," Mrs. Grant said, and her voice was as light and merry as a fountain. "And now Lee's going through that gawky phase, with the braces and all, so you might not even recognize him now."

Mr. President? Was this *the* president? Was Luke shaking the hand of the man who'd outlawed third children? Only disbelief kept Luke from recoiling.

"Oh, I'd recognize this boy anywhere," the man—the president?—said, chuckling. "Looks just like his lovely mother."

Luke choked back something like a giggle.

"And he'd certainly recognize *you*," Mrs. Grant said in a voice so clogged with flattery that Luke could have gagged. "The last time we drove into the city, there were pictures of you everywhere."

"Well," the man said. "People keep insisting on pasting those pictures up. I don't even know where they get them."

"Your people love you," Mrs. Grant said soothingly.

So it was the president. In a daze, Luke shook the next hand that was thrust at him, while Smits shook the president's. Fortunately, no one seemed to expect him to say anything more than, "Hello, sir." And just as fortunately, after the first few people, somehow Smits got ahead of Luke. More than once he turned back to Luke and said something like, "Look, it's the Hadley-Perkinses!"

So Smits was helping Luke once again. Luke wasn't sure how long it would last. And no matter how hard he tried to act normal, he couldn't help glancing up every time he neared a chandelier. There was one in the entryway, one in the living room, one in the parlor—after a while Luke lost count.

And there was Oscar, constantly threading his way behind them like a dark shadow.

Was Oscar waiting for Luke to turn around and announce, "Okay, I've decided. I'll help you now"?

Or was it already too late?

Finally Smits and Luke reached the end of the row of hands they had to shake. The guests seemed to have forgotten them. They stood together off to the side. Luke finally had a chance to think. He nudged Oscar's side.

"Did you see the president?" he asked. "What if we—"

Oscar instantly clapped his hand over Luke's mouth.

"Don't even finish that sentence," he hissed warningly in Luke's ear. "There are guards everywhere."

And then Oscar released him and nodded at a man in a dark suit nearby.

"Just showing him some bodyguard moves," Oscar said calmly.

Luke wasn't even sure what he'd intended to suggest to Oscar. But how could Oscar, who wanted to overthrow the Government, stand in the same room with the president and not do *something*? How could Luke?

Then Luke looked around and noticed how many of the supposed guests had tiny wires leading into their ears, how many men kept their hands over pockets that, for all Luke knew, must have contained guns. Oscar was right—the house was crawling with guards.

Did that make the party safer or more dangerous for Luke?

"Hors d'oeuvres, sir?" a familiar voice said behind him.

A serving girl in a black dress and frilly apron held out a tray full of unidentifiable round food. Luke's face instantly lit up—not because of the food, but because of the girl. It was his friend Nina, who'd gone to the girls' school that bordered Hendricks School for Boys.

Forgetting himself, Luke blurted out, "What are you doing here?"

Nina did a better job of staying in character.

"I was just hired today, sir," she said with a small curtsy. "Mistress hired several new servants just for tonight's party. Me and Trey, and Joel and John . . . we're here to help, sir."

And Luke understood that she meant the last part completely, not just as part of her act. Luke's friends were there to help him. Not just Nina, but Trey and Joel and John. Mr. Hendricks had not sent him off to the Grants' and forgotten about him. For the first time that night Luke felt like beaming.

One of the round cheese balls or sausage balls or whatever they were rolled off Nina's tray. She bent down to pick it up, then glared up at Luke. Luke got the message. He fell to his knees as well and pretended to reach for the food. Nina leaned over and whispered in his ear, "Be careful. Most of the servants are on Oscar's side. And you better believe it's killing me to call you 'sir.'"

"That's good to know," Luke murmured solemnly.

Above him Mrs. Grant swooped in out of nowhere.

"Lee!" she hissed. "Let the servant get that! My son should not be crawling around on the floor during my party!"

"Yes, Mom," Luke said obediently, and stood up.

Mrs. Grant sniffed and steered him over to meet someone whose hand he'd somehow missed shaking.

While he was smiling and nodding and trying to act polite, he caught a glimpse of Trey opening and shutting the door to admit more guests. He saw John stacking dirty plates on a tray and whisking them away. And he saw Oscar, with narrowed eyes, talking to one of the president's guards.

The party, Luke realized, was a battlefield. The sides were being drawn in the midst of the women in their glittering dresses, the men in tuxedos holding elegant champagne glasses, the servants arranging tiny cakes in neat rows on doilies. Luke could guess at the alliances of every person in the room.

Except Smits.

The younger boy was slumped on a sofa, not even looking at the guests talking around him. Luke wondered how the younger boy felt, sitting there ignored, while Mrs. Grant crowed over Luke, "And Lee, you have to meet . . ."

Luke wished he'd been able to tell Smits, just once, how sorry he was that Smits had lost his brother.

But would Smits have believed him?

CHAPTER **TWENTY-EIGHT**

By the time the first guests started leaving, hours later, Luke felt like he'd shaken hundreds of hands, said "sir" and "ma'am" thousands of times, nodded and smiled so much that the muscles in his face ached and the inside of his lips were raw from rubbing on the braces. He'd gone glassy-eyed from forcing himself to stare directly into the faces of total strangers. And his right arm ached from the vise grip Mrs. Grant kept on it, guiding him from guest to guest.

"The president is about to leave," she hissed in his ear. "We must go outside and bid him farewell. It's protocol."

Smits came, too, this time. The three Grants and Luke walked outside and lined up as a chauffeur drove the presidential car around to the front. Mr. and Mrs. Grant stood practically shoulder to shoulder, with Smits on Mrs. Grant's right and Luke on Mr. Grant's left. A cool breeze blew through Luke's hair, and he heard a faint tinkling overhead. He looked up—right at the enormous chandelier he'd been amazed by when he'd first arrived at the Grants' house.

Luke shivered. The blazing lights seemed to blur as he fought back panic. *Watch out for chandeliers. . . .* It was all he could do not to bolt immediately. But all the guests were watching him. *The Grants won't try to fake my death if they're standing under the chandelier with me,* he thought. *And Oscar won't try to fake Smits's death if I'm here, too.* He forced himself to stand still and straight and tall, an arrogant Grant just like Smits and his parents. But out of the corner of his eye he kept track of where his friends were—Trey just behind him, off to the left, and Nina and Joel and John in a clump of servants watching through a side door as the president departed. And he noted that Oscar was just behind Smits. *Oscar's not going to endanger himself,* Luke told himself.

The president stepped out of the house. His chauffeur opened the door of his limousine and stood waiting as the president slowly moved toward the Grants. He shook each of their hands in turn and gave Mrs. Grant a kiss on each cheek.

"Marvelous party as usual, Sarinia," the president said. And then, as the chauffeur was helping the president into his car, Luke heard Nina scream behind him.

"Watch out!"

Instinctively Luke looked up. The chandelier was shaking, swaying ominously back and forth. Luke had time to move, but he couldn't suddenly—his muscles seemed frozen in fear. And then, just as the chandelier began plunging toward him, Luke felt someone knock him off his feet.

It was Trey. Trey had tackled him.

They landed safely off to the side just as the chandelier smashed down in a huge explosion of breaking glass. The blazing lights were extinguished instantly. Luke felt shards spray out against his bare hand, practically the only part of his body that wasn't sheltered by Trey. The braces bit into his lip and he tasted blood in his mouth. Somebody screamed, and then there was silence. Luke was scared to look back at the chandelier, but he glanced up at the circle of guests and servants around him, silhouetted in the dimmer lights from the windows. Everyone stood frozen in horror.

"That's what you get for teaching me how to play football," Trey said in Luke's ear.

"You saved my life," Luke muttered back. "You're the hero tonight."

"Yeah," Trey said, sounding amazed. "I guess I am."

And then he inched away gingerly, being careful not to touch any of the broken glass. His cheeks and hands were already bleeding.

Luke didn't get up yet, but he gathered the nerve to turn his head to the side, toward the fallen chandelier. Incredibly, Smits was standing out of the way, totally unscathed. But he was staring at the heap of shattered glass with an unearthly look on his face.

"Dead," he wailed. "They're all dead! My brother is dead!

My parents are dead! Oh, my . . . brother . . . is . . . dead!"

Luke scrambled to his feet so quickly that he accidentally drove more slivers of glass into his hands. He didn't bother to brush them away. He stood looking across the ruined chandelier at the younger boy.

"I'm alive, Smits," he said. "As long as I'm alive, you have a brother."

If he'd just wanted to keep up the charade of being Lee, he would have spoken differently. But he was too shocked to think about charades or pretenses or lies that had to be told. He was just trying to comfort Smits.

"I'm your brother, Smits," he said. And Smits looked past all the shattered glass and nodded.

CHAPTER TWENTY-NINE

The other people seemed to awaken from their trance after that. The president's chauffeur slammed the door behind the president, scurried into the front seat of the car, and zoomed away, leaving behind dozens of guards. The guards began screaming into mouthpieces, "Alert! Alert! Someone tried to assassinate the president!" They yelled at the horrified guests, "This residence is locked down immediately! Nobody shall leave until we discover who perpetrated this heinous crime!"

Luke looked around. He saw the fear in the faces of Nina and Trey, Joel and John. If they were subjected to lengthy interrogations, would they be able to tell the lies they were supposed to tell? For that matter, could he? And what would Oscar say?

Luke stepped forward. He tried to swagger every bit as much as Smits had when he'd first arrived at Hendricks. He tried to sound every bit as pompous and powerful as Mr. Grant.

"This is ridiculous," he said to the man who appeared to be the head guard. "Nobody was trying to assassinate the president. He didn't get so much as a scratch. It was my parents who died, and my brother and I who barely escaped with our lives, in this tragic accident. And it had to have been an accident. Who could have planned to have an eight-hundred-pound chandelier topple at the exact right moment? And you want to hold an investigation now, here, at the site of my parents' tragic death? When they're still, um, buried there?" He pointed toward the broken chandelier. He was trying to sound grief stricken and horrified, like a boy who had just seen his parents killed. Surprisingly, it wasn't hard. "I—my brother and I— we are the heirs to the Grant family fortune. And we say to you—you are no longer welcome on our property. Leave! Now!"

The head guard stared back at Luke. His eyes said, very clearly, *You're just a punk kid. I don't have to do a thing you say. How do I know you weren't the one who set this up just to get your parents' fortune?* But then he stepped back and seemed to be taking in the mood of the crowd. People were beginning to mutter, "He's right. How can you be so cruel to those poor orphans?" and "I'm a Baron. You're not going to interrogate *me*." And then Luke saw fear in the guard's eyes, too.

"All right," the guard said. "We'll just take everyone's names and conduct the investigation later, as we see fit."

The guests began to slip away then, the women somehow

managing to rush on their tottering high heels, the men so eager to leave that they drove off through the grass or squealed their tires on the pavement. Luke noticed that no matter how warmly the guests had talked to the Grants only moments earlier, no one bothered to stop and console Smits and Luke, no one hesitated even long enough to say, "I'm really going to miss my friends. I'm so sorry that they're dead."

Everyone was scared.

Finally all the guards and guests were gone. Luke had been standing numbly, watching the dozens of taillights depart. Reluctantly he turned around and found a hundred eyes staring straight at him. The servants were waiting for their orders. And now, improbably, he had become their boss.

Luke wanted to ask, "Who did this? And why?" But he knew he'd hear nothing but lies in response. He wanted to shout out, "Why are you looking at me? Can't someone else take care of this? Can't somebody call Mr. Talbot or Mr. Hendricks?" But there were those special codes blocking all the phones. Nobody else could take charge. Luke swallowed hard, swallowing blood, and began pointing at servants, mostly at random. "You, clean up this mess. You, take care of my parents', um, bodies. You, you, you, and you—clean up from the party."

And all the servants scrambled to do his bidding.

Luke remembered a quote from one of his history books: "The king is dead, long live the king." He'd always thought it was funny before, nonsensical even. But now it made perfect sense. The king and queen of the estate—Mr. and Mrs. Grant—were dead, and now Luke was in charge and everyone wanted to believe that he'd do a good job.

Luke turned around, and out of the blue Oscar was suddenly hugging him.

"You're a good kid, even if you aren't ready to work with me yet," he said in Luke's ear, barely loud enough for Luke to hear. "We were aiming for the president, but we held off so we didn't hit you. You owe me now."

Somehow Luke couldn't believe that. It didn't make sense. He would have been dead if Trey hadn't saved him. Oscar was just trying to manipulate Luke again, trying to turn a mistake into an obligation.

"And I owe you for sending the guards away," Oscar said. "Here's my thanks."

Luke felt something fall into his pant pocket. But it wasn't until Oscar had released him and walked away that Luke could gather his wits enough to reach in and find out what it was.

His fingers brushed smooth metal, then teeth. It was a key.

Luke knew instantly what the key unlocked.

"Smits, come with me," Luke said. "Nina, Trey—you, too. And Joel and John—you two are in charge while I'm away."

He gave them some quick instructions. Joel and John nodded numbly. This was a lot more important than leaving them in charge of the nightly games at Hendricks School, and they hadn't seemed confident enough to handle that. But it couldn't be helped.

Luke led Smits, Trey, and Nina through a maze of rooms that almost seemed familiar now. In front of the secret room he didn't even bother to look around to see who might be watching. He just thrust the key in—yes, it was the right key—and let his friends into the dark room. Luke began to fumble with the controls on the wall, but Smits took over, punching the right sequence to turn on the lights and seal the door.

"Lee and I," he said. "We used to come here sometimes, to hide. To make secret plans. Silly things like dropping water balloons on the cooks. Putting sneezing powder in our beds for the maids when they cleaned our rooms. We had so much fun before—before he died."

He looked around dazedly, as if he'd forgotten that he was speaking aloud.

"Oh, sorry, I didn't know there were servants here. You can't believe a word I say," he told Trey and Nina. "I'm crazy. Everyone thinks so."

"No, you're not," Luke said. "And it's okay to tell the truth now. Trey and Nina are my friends."

"Oh. Yes. Trey. I remember you. What are you doing here?"

"Helping out," Trey said. Smits's stunned expression didn't change.

"I think he's in shock," Nina whispered to Luke. But Smits heard her.

"No," he said. "I think I was in shock for the past six months. But now I'm—am I free now? Is Oscar gone?"

Luke remembered the way Oscar had hugged him, the way he'd slipped off into the darkness.

"I think so," Luke said.

Smits eased down into one of the chairs and stared bleakly at the wall.

"I didn't think he would kill *them*," Smits said, almost as if he was talking to himself. "He said he would destroy you." Slowly he raised his head until his empty gaze was fixed on Luke.

"M-me?" Luke stammered.

"He wanted me to help," Smits said without emotion. "Because you weren't Lee. Because you'd taken his name. Because you weren't a Baron. Oscar was a Baron, did you know that? He was just pretending to be a servant. To get revenge."

Luke's jaw dropped. "What? Oscar wasn't a Baron! He hated Barons!"

Smits didn't seem to hear Luke.

"I wouldn't help him," Smits said. "Not when it mattered. I helped you, just to make him mad. Is that . . . is that why Oscar killed them? Because I wouldn't do what he said?"

Tears began to flow down his face. He brushed them away, leaving smears of blood on his cheeks. His hands must have been bleeding, and none of them had noticed.

"Oscar was trying to kill the president," Luke said. "Not your parents. He just . . . missed."

But Luke wasn't sure that he believed that. How could he believe anything Oscar had told him?

"People try to kill my parents all the time," Smits said. "Lee and me, we weren't supposed to know, but—remember when the flaming dessert exploded? That was one time. . . . And there was a bomb once, in my dad's office. . . . But Mom and Dad, they always survived. Somehow. Maybe"—his face lit up, and he sat forward—"maybe they aren't dead now. Maybe they're just hurt really bad, and if we have the servants take them to the hospital . . ."

Luke thought about the pile of broken glass, of the way that Mr. and Mrs. Grant's bodies hadn't even been visible beneath the wreckage.

"No," he said gently. "They're dead."

Smits slumped back in his seat, back into stony silence.

"How did Oscar do it?" Nina asked. "How did he get the chandelier to fall when he was standing practically underneath it? If there'd been someone up there cutting the wires, someone Oscar was commanding, we would have seen him."

Luke hadn't even thought about that. The chandelier's falling had seemed like a tornado or an earthquake—something so sudden and cataclysmic that it didn't make sense to look for explanations.

"It was some sort of remote-control hookup," Trey said. "I bet if we looked, we'd find a release on the wires that went off when Oscar gave a signal. Or maybe he pressed the button himself. Maybe nobody except Oscar knew what was going to happen."

Luke remembered Oscar's warning: "Watch out for chandeliers." Oscar apparently hadn't given Smits the same warning. Even after Luke had refused to take sides, even after the chandelier had fallen, Oscar still seemed to have held on to some hope that Luke might join his cause. "You're a good kid, even if you aren't ready to work with me yet," Oscar had said. The "yet" kept ringing in Luke's ears.

Especially now Luke couldn't imagine ever joining forces with Oscar. Had he made a mistake, letting Oscar slip off into the darkness? Luke buried his face in his hands. His mind raced. How could he ever sort out the truth from Oscar's lies? Oscar had tried to get both Smits and Luke to help him. But it was Luke he'd given the warning to, Luke he'd hugged, Luke he'd left with the key. . . . Luke could almost feel certain: Oscar probably had been poor. He probably had blown up mailboxes. He probably did hate Barons—including the Grants.

"Smits?" Luke said gently, looking up again. "How did Oscar act around your parents?"

Smits blinked.

"Act?" he repeated, as though he'd misunderstood the question. "Yeah, it was all an act. Everything he did. He'd be all nice to them—all, 'Yes, Mrs. Grant. No, Mr. Grant.' But he was—was blackmailing them. The whole time."

"What?" Luke exploded. "It was Oscar doing that?" He'd

never suspected such a thing, but somehow it fit.

Smits didn't even seem to hear Luke. He kept talking, as if in a trance.

"They didn't know it was him," Smits said. "But I found . . . I found a check in his wallet. From them. Not his bodyguard pay. He was writing them letters, saying he knew that Lee was dead and how he had died. And he was going to tell the Government if they didn't pay up. . . ."

"Didn't you tell your parents what he was doing?" Trey asked.

"No," Smits said. His expression twisted with guilt. "I thought . . . I thought they were getting what they deserved." He was silent for a minute, then went on angrily, "They didn't even want to tell *me* that Lee was dead. 'Oh, he's too busy to answer your E-mail,' they said. 'Oh, he's just out when you call.' 'Oh, he's having too much fun to come and see his pesky little brother.'"

Luke could understand why Smits had been so upset.

"But you did find out about Lee," Nina said gently.

Smits nodded. "Lee wasn't like that. He didn't think I was pesky. He took care of me. *He* loved me. So I knew something was wrong. I started spying on Mom and Dad. And I caught Mom in here, crying. And then I made her tell me, and she made me promise to keep everything secret, but . . . I couldn't, you know? And I kept thinking, Mom was crying over Lee. And I didn't think she would cry if I died. But then tonight, when that chandelier started to fall—Mom pushed me out of the way. She saved my life. And she didn't have time to save her own. She—she must have loved me after all. And now—now I don't have any parents at all. . . ."

Smits began crying then, really hard. Awkwardly Luke patted his shoulders. Nina bent down and hugged him. Trey, who clearly wasn't any good around emotional outbursts, drifted over toward Mr. Grant's desk. He began rifling through the drawers. After a few moments Luke joined him.

"It'd be nice if we could find some papers—some proof," Trey muttered. "We can't believe what Smits tells us, can we?"

Luke glanced back at the sobbing boy.

"Yeah," he said. "He's too sad to lie."

Luke was convinced: Smits definitely believed everything he'd told them was true. He'd mostly told the truth all along—until Oscar had begun pressuring him to betray Luke, as a way to betray his parents. Smits's only lies were the ones that had come from other people.

Luke was willing to stand there and try to figure everything out, but Trey elbowed him in the ribs.

"Where'd you get the key to this room?" he asked.

"Oscar gave it to me," Luke said absentmindedly.

"How do we know he hasn't bugged the whole place?" Trey asked. "How do we know he isn't still planning to kill you and Smits?"

Luke stared at his friend. Luke's vision was starting to go fuzzy around the edges. It was so tempting to give in to that fuzziness, to slump down in a heap and let someone else figure out what to do. But he blinked hard, blinking Trey and the secret room back into focus. And Nina and Smits.

Most of all Smits.

"Think one of us can figure out how to drive?" Luke asked.

CHAPTER THIRTY

In the end they decided to trust the chauffeur. Joel and John sat in the front with him, ready to overpower him if he tried anything suspicious.

Trey and Luke sat in the first seat in the back, all the papers from Mr. Grant's desk spread out between them. Trey had insisted on bringing them. He was methodically reading one paper after the other with a penlight. Occasionally he'd mutter, "This is incredible!" or "Listen to this!" but Luke barely heard him. It was always something financial, something about Mr. Grant's business. Nothing Luke cared about. Luke just stared straight ahead, thinking.

Nina and Smits sat across from Luke and Trey. Or lay, in Smits's case. He'd fallen asleep leaning against Nina, but he still whimpered and thrashed about. Several times she had to grab him to keep him from falling off the seat.

Every time that happened, Luke knew he was doing the right thing.

It had been the middle of the night when they started out, so their entire trip had been in darkness. There seemed to be no light at all in the world except in their car. But by the time Trey finally gave up on the papers and turned off his penlight, the first gleam of dawn had begun creeping over the horizon. Luke stopped staring at Smits and began pressing his face against the window, trying to see something familiar outside. He couldn't get enough of staring at the landscape around him.

When the car passed a crossroads with nothing but three mailboxes in the midst of a clump of weeds, he suddenly screamed out, "Stop!"

The chauffeur hit the brakes so hard that Smits finally rolled completely off his seat.

"Sorry, sir," the chauffeur said.

"That's all right," Luke said. "You can let Smits and me out here."

"Here?" The man sounded incredulous. Luke saw him looking around at rutted fields stretching all the way to the horizon. To the chauffeur and almost anyone else who might see this scene, it would look like a vast wasteland. The middle of nowhere.

But that wasn't what Luke saw.

"You can take the others on to Mr. Talbot's house," Luke said. "Thanks."

Luke didn't wait for the chauffeur to open the door for him. He pushed his way out on his own.

"Come on, Smits," he said gently, holding the door.

Nina handed the younger boy over as if he were a mere parcel. Still, Smits stood up straight once he was out of the car. Luke saw him glance down at the dried mud streaked across the road, but he didn't say anything.

"You won't change your mind?" Trey asked. "You can still come with the rest of us."

"No," Luke said. "I've got to do it this way."

He had a feeling Mr. Talbot would disapprove. He was probably being a coward, not going to Mr. Talbot's house first. Or foolhardy for not discussing everything with Mr. Talbot before making up his mind. But Luke knew now that Mr. Talbot didn't know everything, either. Mr. Talbot was going to be stunned to learn what Oscar had done. Luke was perfectly willing to let Trey and Nina break the news.

"Okay," Trey said hesitantly.

Luke shoved the door shut and turned to Smits.

"Up ahead," Luke said. "That house. That's where we're going."

They waited until the car drove out of sight, then they began walking. Luke barely managed to keep himself from breaking into a run—he was that eager. But he had the younger boy to think about, and Smits didn't seem capable of running right now.

Finally they reached the driveway, and Luke could restrain himself no longer. He raced up to the door and pounded.

"Mother! Dad! I'm home!"

The door flew open and Mother stood there, her jaw dropped in astonishment.

"Oh, Lu—," she began, then swallowed the rest of his name and just buried him in a hug. Then she stopped and held him out from her by the shoulders, much as Mrs. Grant had held him when she was planning all the ways to change him. But Mrs. Grant had been looking for his faults, and Mother was beaming as though everything about him was wonderful.

"You've gotten taller and more muscular, and your hair's darker and—are those braces?" she asked in amazement. She didn't wait for an answer. Her face clouded suddenly, as though she'd just remembered why he'd had to leave home in the first place. "Is it safe for you to be here?" she asked.

"As safe as anywhere else," Luke replied steadily. For that, finally, was what he'd concluded. Oscar knew about Hendricks School and Mr. Talbot, the Grants' house was a Byzantine mess of mixed loyalties—if Luke was going to be in danger, he might as well get to see his family. And he wasn't going to be staying long enough to endanger them.

"Everything's different now, Mother," he said. But he couldn't say to her, "I just saw two people killed, right before my eyes. I was almost killed myself. And then the murderer hugged me. . . . How can anything stay the same after that?"

Mother gave him a searching look and opened her mouth as if she was going to ask more. But Smits reached the front door just then, a sad, slow little boy who seemed to have barely enough energy to climb the steps. Luke saw the sympathy playing over his mother's face. She didn't even know what had happened to Smits, and she already felt sorry for him.

Good.

"Mother, remember how you always wanted to have four boys?" Luke asked. "Well, I brought you another son. This is Smits. Smits Grant. He is—was—well, he's my brother now. His parents are dead."

Automatically Smits held out a hand, and for a single second Luke felt a stab of doubt. Mother and Smits looked so wrong together—like pictures cut from two different magazines and haphazardly glued together. Smits, in his fine woolen suit and leather shoes, did not belong with Mother, with her faded housedress and haggard face, her graying hair scooped back into a bun. And what had Luke been thinking, bringing Smits from his mansion to Luke's family's house, with its peeling paint and weathered wood? What must Smits think?

Mother ignored Smits's outstretched hand and drew him into a hug that was every bit as genuine as the one she'd given Luke.

"You're always welcome here," she told him.

Then Luke's dad and older brothers, Matthew and Mark, came out to see what the fuss was about. They weren't the type to give hugs, but Luke could see the joy and relief in their eyes, even as Matthew punched his arm and Mark joked, "Luke? You couldn't be Luke. I could always whomp Luke with one hand tied behind my back. And you—with you I might have to use both fists."

That was how Luke knew that Mark was happier than anyone to see him.

They all shook hands politely with Smits. Luke could tell they were shy around him.

"Have you had breakfast? We were just getting ready to sit down," Mother said.

"I could eat," Smits said in a small voice.

Matthew and Mark brought in extra chairs from the other rooms, and they all sat around the kitchen table. Such a change, Luke thought, from when he'd had to eat on the stairs while the rest of the family ate at the table. Breakfast was just oatmeal and cooked apples, but it tasted heavenly to Luke, better than the fanciest meal he'd had at the Grants'.

He wondered what Smits thought.

After breakfast everyone sat around talking, until Mother had to scurry off to work, and Matthew and Mark had to rush off to school.

"Are we going to have to put up with you when we get home, too?" Mark asked, just as the school bus pulled up.

"Probably," Luke said. "Today, at least."

"Too bad," Mark said, but Luke could tell he was secretly glad.

With the others out the door, Luke's dad asked them, "Mind if I turn on the radio? I have to check the grain report."

It was so odd that Dad would ask Luke permission for anything. Luke watched Dad twist the radio dial, and the familiar voice of the news announcer crackled out of the speaker.

"Government spokesmen report record harvests this year," the announcer said.

Luke remembered the empty fields he'd seen going from school to the Grants' house, from the Grants' house to home. He remembered all the lies he'd witnessed since leaving home in the first place. Even if the news announcer's voice was the same as ever, Luke couldn't listen unquestioningly, the way he once had. He wondered suddenly if anything the Government told the people was true.

Beside him Smits sniffled.

"They aren't . . . they aren't saying anything about Mom and Dad," he said.

"No," Luke said gently. "They wouldn't." He remembered how he'd longed to hear news on the radio about Jen, Mr. Talbot's daughter, after her rally but before he knew what had really happened. "It's better for you if they don't announce it," he told Smits.

"But I can talk about it, can't I?" Smits asked.

"Yes," Luke said. "Here you can say anything you want."

Smits fell silent then. Luke understood. But Dad glanced from Smits to Luke, his eyebrows furrowed in confusion.

"Is there something I ought to know?" Dad asked.

"Later," Luke mouthed, cutting his eyes toward Smits in

a quiet signal: *Not in front of the little boy.* Luke realized that his parents, and even Matthew and Mark, had done that around Luke all those years he'd lived at home. They'd protected him. He'd been the little boy. And now Luke was protecting Smits.

Luke half expected Dad to ask more, but he just nodded and turned back to the radio news.

"Come on," Luke said to Smits. "I'll show you around."

They stepped out the kitchen door into the backyard. Luke froze, staring out at the barn and the trees and the garden, now dried up and dying. Once, this yard had practically been Luke's whole world. Once, it had seemed huge and endless, especially when he'd been gathering the nerve to run across it to see Jen. But now—now it seemed tiny. Luke felt like he could cross the distance to the Talbots' backyard in a few quick strides.

Smits sat down on the back step.

"Your family loves you," he said. "They missed you while you were away."

"Yes," Luke said.

"I wish my parents had . . . ," Smits started, but he choked on the rest of the words and stopped. Luke patted him on the back and sat down beside him.

"My parents will take care of you now," Luke said. "Is that okay?"

After a few seconds Smits nodded. Luke slipped his hand into his pocket and pulled out the I.D. that claimed Smits was really Peter Goodard.

"Do you want this?" Luke asked. "I found it in your room at school, after the fire. I didn't know what Oscar was going to do with it, but—"

"Oscar? He didn't know anything about it," Smits said.

"What?" Just when Luke thought he had everything figured out, another surprise cropped up.

"You found it in his mattress, right?" Smits said. "I hid it there because I thought that was the one place he wouldn't look. Oscar—he searched everything I owned. Every day. He had ways of finding out everything."

He took the I.D. from Luke and clutched it in his hand.

"But that first day you came to Hendricks—you had tricked Oscar then," Luke said. "You'd locked him in the closet."

Smits flashed Luke a disgusted look. "Oscar planned all that. He set me up. He thought I'd get to Hendricks and make some big scene and betray you, and betray my—my parents. . . ."

"Why didn't you?" Luke asked.

Smits stared at the ground. "When I met you and had to call you Lee, it was like, just saying his name—I thought, what if you could be Lee? I mean, I knew you weren't really Lee, but . . . you kind of look like him. A little. And I thought maybe . . . You listened to me. Like Lee used to. But other times I would be so mad at you, and I was mean to you because . . ."

"Because I wasn't Lee," Luke finished. "Not for real."

Smits nodded.

And from that garbled explanation Luke somehow understood how it had been for Smits. He'd had no one he could trust. His brother was dead and Luke was using his name. So of course he was angry. But he'd also let himself drop into fantasy. "Can you be Lee?" Smits had asked Luke that on his very first day at Hendricks. And Luke had wondered what Smits really meant, what code Luke was supposed to understand. But Smits had meant exactly what he'd said. He'd wanted Luke to be Lee. Nothing more, nothing less.

Luke shook his head, trying to make sense of all this new information.

"But—the fire," he said. "Why did you set the fire if— and why didn't you take the I.D. when—"

"Oscar set the fire," Smits said. "Or—it was his idea. Just from what I told you that night, he figured out that I was planning to run away."

So Oscar had been listening the whole time, all those nights Smits had reminisced about Lee. And Smits might have escaped if he hadn't told Luke, "None of this is because of you. It won't be your fault. I even . . . I even kind of like you." Everything would have been different if Smits hadn't cared about Luke.

But maybe—maybe everything would have been worse instead of better. Maybe Smits would be dead now, too.

"But why did you want to run away?" Luke asked. "Where were you going to go?"

"Where I could find out more about Lee," Smits said. "I

wanted to talk to people who'd seen him right before he died. Oscar said he'd help me if I could make it look like it wasn't his fault for letting me go. Like he'd been too busy fighting the fire and saving my life to keep me from leaving. So I lit the matches, and he held his hands over the sprinklers as long as he could. . . . I thought Oscar would leave and I could grab the I.D. at the last minute. But the fire took off faster than I'd thought, and that teacher came in, Mr. Dirk. I think Oscar just wanted Mr. Hendricks to send us home, where he could make more trouble. He—he got what he wanted."

Luke was trying to sort everything out. "So you thought Oscar would help you? Why did you act like you didn't trust him?"

Smits looked weary. "Because I didn't. There were so many lies. I didn't know what to believe. Sometimes I believed him, sometimes I didn't."

Luke shivered, remembering his own confusion about Oscar. He could sympathize with Smits, trying to cope with Oscar's lies and manipulations for so long.

"I think I understand everything now," Luke said. "Except—where did you get the fake I.D. in the first place? And this other one—whose was it if it wasn't Oscar's?"

Luke drew out the pictureless I.D. for Stanley Goodard. Smits didn't look surprised to see it. He reached out and touched it gently.

"Lee's," he said. He stared out at the leafless trees at the edge of the yard.

"Lee knew there was danger," Smits said. "He said our country was going to change, and it might not be safe anymore for us. . . . So he gave me the fake I.D., just in case. He showed me that he had a fake I.D. of his own. And then he left."

"So how did you get Lee's?" Luke asked.

"I stole it from Dad's desk," Smits said, and gave Luke a defiant look, just daring him to tell Smits that stealing was wrong.

Luke didn't.

"So this was the identification Lee was carrying when he died," Luke said. That fake I.D. was what made it safe for Luke to pretend to be Lee. The Government soldiers would never have known that they'd killed the real Lee Grant.

"The resistance group must have given it to your parents," Luke said. "As proof."

Smits shrugged, as though none of those details mattered.

"But what happened to the picture?" Luke asked.

In answer Smits reached inside his shirt and peeled a small, battered piece of clear tape off his chest. He held it out to Luke.

"Mom and Dad got rid of all the pictures of Lee," Smits said. "For protection, they said. So—this is all I have."

The tape—badly bent and grubby—was stuck to a picture of a boy who looked vaguely like an older, darker-haired version of Smits. Luke gingerly took the taped picture from Smits and studied it. It was hard to tell anything from such a small picture.

"You've been carrying this around for a long time, haven't you?" Luke asked, carefully handing it back.

Smits nodded.

"I won't have to keep it with me all the time now, will I?" Smits asked.

"No," Luke said.

"But if I put it down, that won't mean I'm forgetting Lee."

"Of course not," Luke said. "You'll never forget him. And I won't, either. And someday it'll be safe to tell the whole world what really happened to Lee. How brave he was and what he believed in."

But even saying that, Luke knew that he'd never truly be sure what the real Lee had believed. Had he joined the rebels, as Oscar said, simply to get revenge on his parents? Had he been as nonchalant as Oscar about harming innocent people? Or had he been a true believer, longing to extend freedom to everyone?

Luke couldn't blame Smits for always wanting more answers about the dead. Luke would probably never know, either, if Mr. and Mrs. Grant had intended to kill him for real or if they'd just meant to send him back into hiding. If they'd wanted to kill him, how could he mourn their death?

But how could he hate them as Oscar did, when they'd given him Lee's identity?

Smits didn't seem to notice Luke's confusion. He bent the tape over the back of the picture and tucked it and the two fake I.D.'s into his pocket. Then he glanced back at Luke.

"Luke? After the chandelier—after it fell, when I yelled, 'My brother is dead,' I didn't mean to betray you. I don't think that anyone understood. But—it felt good, you know? To finally tell the truth, out loud, in front of lots of people. I feel . . . I feel better about Lee now."

"You didn't betray me," Luke said. He wondered how good it would feel for everyone to finally tell the truth. Someday he and Trey and Nina and all his other friends could stand up proud and finally tell the whole world their true names, their true stories. But somehow, even now, sometimes truth slipped out in the midst of all the lies and confusion. "And I really meant it when I said you were my brother now."

"I know," Smits said. "But you're not going to stay with me here, are you?"

It was amazing, Luke thought, that Smits had figured that out. That Smits realized that Luke, like Lee, couldn't make it his top priority to be Smits's brother.

"No," Luke said. "But you'll be safe here. You'll be ordinary old Peter Goodard, whoever that is. It's good that Mr. Hendricks is the only other person who ever saw that I.D. We can make up a story about you, about why you're here. And you don't look like the rest of the family, so no one will think that you're actually a third child with a fake I.D." He almost said, "Like they would if I stayed." But he swallowed those words and smiled at Smits. "You'll have Matthew and Mark. They're horrible brothers, but—well, they're better than nothing. And I'll stay tonight. But then tomorrow—"

"I know," Smits said.

Tomorrow Luke would march across that tiny backyard that separated his family's house from Mr. Talbot's. And then the chauffeur would take him back to the Grants' house or back to Hendricks School or maybe even someplace else. Wherever he went, there'd be danger. But there would also be a chance to work toward that day of truth he longed for.

"Hey," Luke said. "I've got an idea."

He went in the side door of the barn and emerged with a rusty old wagon.

"It's not red, and I'm not Lee, but—I made you a promise."

And Luke sat down in the little kiddie wagon. His knees were practically in his ears. Smits laughed and stood up, then grabbed the handle and pulled. Luke instantly tipped over onto the ground.

"Wow," he said. "No wonder Lee never let you pull."

They goofed off with the wagon for a long time after that, taking turns jerking on the handle and sitting in the wagon. It became a game to see who could stay in the wagon the longest, who could dump the other boy the fastest. Luke's dad came out and stood on the step and laughed at them.

"Here," he said, "I'll pull you both."

And Luke and Smits piled into the wagon, barely fitting in. Luke's dad tugged hard, and for just a minute Luke could believe again that he was just a little kid letting a grown-up determine which way he should go. But then he was on the ground again, and his dad was groaning and rubbing his arm.

"You're too heavy together," he complained jokingly. "Just the little guy this time."

And Luke stood back and watched Smits play with Luke's dad. Smits wasn't a Grant anymore, and Luke was. But now Smits would have Luke's parents, and Luke wouldn't. Luke knew he'd made a bad trade. And with all that he'd risked, he still hadn't done anything grand for the cause.

But he'd helped Smits. And for now that was enough.

Turn the page to read an excerpt from the
fifth book in the Shadow Children sequence

Among
the Brave

MARGARET PETERSON HADDIX

CHAPTER ONE

Great, Trey thought. *I do one brave thing in my entire life, and now it's like, 'Got anything dangerous to do? Send Trey. He can handle it.' Doesn't anyone remember that Cowardice is my middle name?*

Actually, only two other people in the entire world had ever known Trey's real name, and one of them was dead. But Trey didn't have time to think about that. He had a crisis on his hands. He'd just seen two people killed, and others in danger. Maybe he'd been in danger too. Maybe he still was. He and his friends had left the scene of all that death and destruction and total confusion, jumped into a car with an absolute stranger, and rushed off in search of help. They'd driven all night, and now the car had stopped in front of a strange house in a strange place Trey had never been before.

And Trey's friends actually expected him to take control of the situation.

"What are you waiting for?" his friend Nina asked. "Just go knock on the door."

"Why don't you?" Trey asked, which was as good as admitting that he wasn't as brave as a girl. No courage, no pride. Translate that into Latin and it'd be a good personal motto for him. *Nulla fortitudo nulla superbia,* maybe? Trey allowed himself a moment to drift into nostalgia for the days when his biggest challenges had been figuring out how to translate Latin phrases.

"Because," Nina said. "You know. Mr. Talbot and I—well, let's just say I've got a lot of bad memories."

"Oh," Trey said. And, if he could manage to turn down his fear a notch or two, he did understand. Mr. Talbot, the man they had come to see, had once put Nina through an extreme test of her loyalties. It had been necessary, everyone agreed—even Nina said so. But it hadn't been pleasant. Mr. Talbot had kept her in prison; he'd threatened her with death.

Trey was glad he'd never been put through a test like that. He knew: He'd fail.

Trey glanced up again at the hulking monstrosity of a house where Mr. Talbot lived. He wasn't dangerous, Trey reminded himself. Mr. Talbot was going to be their salvation. Trey and Nina and a few of their other friends had come to Mr. Talbot's so they could dump all their bad news and confusion on him. So he would handle everything, and they wouldn't have to.

Trey peered toward the front of the car, where his friends Joel and John sat with the driver. Or, technically, the "chauffeur," a word derived from the French. Only the original French word—*chauffer?*—didn't mean "to drive." It meant "to warm" or "to heat" or something like that, because chauffeurs used to drive steam automobiles.

Not that it mattered. Why was he wasting time thinking about foreign verbs? Knowing French wasn't going to help Trey in the least right now. It couldn't tell him, for example, whether he could trust the driver. Everything would be so easy if he could know, just from one word, whether he could send the driver to knock on Mr. Talbot's door while Trey safely cowered in the car.

Or how about Joel or John? Granted, they were younger than Trey, and maybe even bigger cowards. They'd *never* done anything brave. Still—

"Trey?" Nina said. *"Go!"*

She reached around him and jerked open the door. Then she gave him a little shove on the back, so suddenly that he was surprised to find himself outside the car, standing on his own two feet.

Nina shut the door behind him.

Trey took a deep breath. He started to clench his fists out of habit and fear—a habit of fear, a fear-filled habit—and only stopped when pain reminded him that he was still clutching the sheaf of papers he'd taken from a dead man's desk. He glanced down and saw a thin line of fresh blood, stark and frightening on the bright white paper.

Trey's next breath was sharp and panicked. Had someone shot him? Was he in even greater danger than he'd imagined? His ears buzzed, and he thought he might pass out from terror. But nothing else happened, and after a few moments his mind cleared a little.

He looked at the blood again. It was barely more than a single drop.

Okay, Trey steadied himself. *You just had a panic attack over a paper cut. Let's not be telling anybody about that, all right?*

A paper cut indoors would have been no big deal. But outdoors—outdoors, the need to *breathe* was enough to panic him.

He forced himself to breathe anyway. And, by sheer dint of will, Trey made himself take a single step forward. And then another. And another.

Mr. Talbot had a long, long walkway between the street and his house, and the chauffeur had inconveniently parked off to the side, under a clump of trees that practically hid the car from the house. Trey considered turning around, getting back into the car, and telling the chauffeur to pull up closer—say, onto the Talbots' front porch. But that would mean retracing his steps, and Trey felt like he'd already come so far.

Maybe even all of three feet.

With part of his mind, Trey knew he was being foolish—a total baby, a chicken, a fear-addled idiot.

It's not my fault, Trey defended himself. *It's all . . . conditioning. I can't help the way I was raised.* And that was the understatement of the year. For most of his thirteen years, Trey hadn't had control over any aspect of his life. He was an illegal third child—the entire Government thought he had no right to exist. So he'd had to hide, from birth until age twelve, in a single room. And then, when he was almost thirteen, when his father died . . .

You don't have time to think about that now, Trey told himself sternly. *Walk.*

He took a few more steps forward, propelled now by a burning anger that he'd never managed to escape. His mind slipped back to a multiple-choice test question he'd been asking himself for more than a year: *Whom do you hate? A) Him; B) Her; C) Yourself?* It never worked to add extra choices: *(D) All of the above; E) A and B; F) A and C; or G) B and C?* Because then the question just became, *Whom do you hate the most?*

Stop it! Trey commanded himself. *Just pretend you're Lee.*

Trey's friend Lee had been an illegal third child like Trey, but Lee had grown up out in the country, on an isolated farm, so he'd been able to spend plenty of time outdoors. He'd almost, Trey thought, grown up normal. As much as Trey feared and hated being outdoors, Lee craved it.

"How can you stand it?" Trey had asked Lee once. "Why aren't you terrified? Don't you ever think about the danger?"

"I guess not," Lee had said, shrugging. "When I'm outdoors I look at the sky and the grass and the trees, and I guess that's all I think about."

Trey looked at the sky and the grass and the trees around him, and all he could think was, *Lee should be here, walking up to Mr. Talbot's door, instead of me.* Lee had been in the car with Trey and Nina and Joel and John until just about ten minutes earlier. But Lee had had the chauffeur drop him and another boy, Smits, off at a crossroads in the middle of nowhere because, Lee had said, "I have to get Smits to safety."

Trey suspected that Lee was taking Smits home, to Lee's parents' house, but Trey was trying very hard not to think that. It was too dangerous. Even thinking about it was dangerous.

And thinking about it made Trey jealous, because Lee still had a home he could go to, and parents who loved him, and Trey didn't.

But Lee would be dead right now if it weren't for me, Trey thought with a strange emotion he barely recognized well enough to name. Pride. He felt proud. And, cowardly Latin motto or no, he had a right to that pride.

For Trey's act of bravery—his only one ever—had been to save Lee's life the night before.

Beneath the pride was a whole jumble of emotions Trey hadn't had time to explore. He felt his leg muscles tense, as if they too remembered last night, remembered springing forward at the last minute to knock Lee to the side, only seconds before the explosion of glass in the very spot where Lee had stood. . . .

It's easier being brave when you don't have time to think about your other options, Trey thought. *Unlike now.*

He had so many choices, out here in the open. The ones that called to him most strongly were the ones that involved hiding. How fast would he be able to run back to the car, if he needed to? Would the clump of trees be a good hiding place? Would he be able to squeeze out of sight between that giant flowerpot on the porch and the wall of the Talbot house?

Trey forced himself to keep walking. It seemed a miracle when he finally reached the front porch. He cast a longing glance toward the flowerpot, but willed himself to stab a finger at the doorbell.

Dimly, he could hear a somber version of "Westminster Chimes" echoing from indoors. Nobody came. He took a second to admire the brass door knocker, elegantly engraved with the words, GEORGE A. TALBOT, ESQUIRE. Still nobody came.

Too bad, Trey thought. *Back to the car, then.* But his legs didn't obey. He couldn't face the thought of walking back through all that open space again. He pressed the doorbell again.

This time the door opened.

Trey was torn between relief and panic. Relief won when he saw Mr. Talbot's familiar face on the other side of the door. *See, this wasn't so bad,* Trey told himself. *I walked all the way up here without my legs even trembling. Take that, Nina! I am braver than you!*

Trey started thinking about what he was supposed to say to Mr. Talbot. He hadn't worried about that before. Words were so much easier than action.

"I'm so glad you're home, Mr. Talbot," Trey began. "You won't believe what happened. We just—"

But Mr. Talbot cut him off.

"No, no, I do not want to buy anything to support your school's lacrosse team," he said. "And please do *not* come back. Tell the rest of your team that this is a no-soliciting house. Can't you see I'm a busy man?"

Mr. Talbot's eyebrows beetled together, like forbidding punctuation.

"But, Mr. Talbot—I'm not—I'm—"

Too late. The door slammed in his face.

"—Trey," Trey finished in a whisper, talking now to the door.

He doesn't remember me, Trey thought. It wasn't that surprising. Every time Mr. Talbot had visited Hendricks School, where Trey and Lee were students, Trey had been in the background, no more noticeable than the wallpaper.

Lee, on the other hand, had been front and center, talking to Mr. Talbot, joking with him, going off for special meals with him.

Mr. Talbot wouldn't have slammed the door in Lee's face, Trey thought. Was Trey jealous of that, too? *No. I just wish Lee were here to talk with Mr. Talbot now.*

Trey sighed, and began gathering the nerve to ring the doorbell again.

But then two things happened, one after the other.

First, a car shot out from under the house—from a hidden garage, Trey guessed. It was black and long and official-looking. Its tires screeched, winding around the curves of the driveway. Trey caught a glimpse of two men in uniforms in the front seat, and Mr. Talbot in the back. Mr. Talbot held up his hands toward the window, toward Trey, and Trey saw a glint of something metal around his wrists.

Handcuffs?

The black car bounced over the curb and then sped off down the street.

Trey was still standing there, his mouth agape, his mind struggling to make sense of what he'd seen, when the car he'd ridden in—the car that Nina, Joel, and John were still hiding in—began to inch forward, under the cover of the trees. Trey felt a second of hope: *They're coming to rescue me!*

But the car was going in the wrong direction.

Trey stared as the car slid away, just a shadow in the trees, then a black streak on the open road.

Then it was gone.

They left me! Trey's mind screamed. *They left me!*

He was all alone on an uncaring man's porch—an arrested man's porch?—out in the great wide open where anyone in the world might see him.

Without thinking, Trey dived behind the huge flowerpot, to hide.